WHERE THERE'S SMOKE

JAYNE RYLON

eBook ISBN: 978-1-941785-43-0
Print ISBN: 978-1-941785-63-8

Cover Art By Jayne Rylon
Interior Print Book Design By Jayne Rylon

OTHER BOOKS BY JAYNE RYLON

DIVEMASTERS
Going Down
Going Deep
Going Hard

MEN IN BLUE
Night is Darkest
Razor's Edge
Mistress's Master
Spread Your Wings
Wounded Hearts
Bound For You

POWERTOOLS
Kate's Crew
Morgan's Surprise
Kayla's Gift
Devon's Pair
Nailed to the Wall
Hammer it Home

HOTRODS
King Cobra
Mustang Sally
Super Nova
Rebel on the Run
Swinger Style
Barracuda's Heart

Touch of Amber
Long Time Coming

Compass Brothers
Northern Exposure
Southern Comfort
Eastern Ambitions
Western Ties

Compass Girls
Winter's Thaw
Hope Springs
Summer Fling
Falling Softly

Play Doctor
Dream Machine
Healing Touch

Standalones
4-Ever Theirs
Nice & Naughty
Where There's Smoke
Report For Booty

Racing For Love
Driven
Shifting Gears

Red Light
Through My Window
Star

Can't Buy Love
Free For All

DEDICATION

For my mom.

Nope, you can't read this one either.

CHAPTER ONE

Kyana Brady roamed the perfectly imperfect old house she'd inherited using only the silver light of the full moon to guide her through the familiar second-story hallway. Her cornflower blue silk and lace nightgown seemed extravagant given that she was all alone, but the luxury helped her survive the night. It reminded her of a time when she'd had money, power and control over her life, not to mention those of the clients who'd depended on her to solve their problems in high-profile legal battles.

Six months ago, those things had seemed like enough.

Her last circuit of the upstairs hallway and the bedroom she'd inhabited as a teenager had given her a chance to debate whether she should email her partners—*ex*-partners—and concede to their relentless begging that she resume her duties. This time around, she paused to stare into Aunt Rose's room, still exactly as the woman had left it the day she'd surrendered to liver cancer a few months earlier.

Time had slipped away without Kyana's usual routines to tick off the passing days with the precision of a metronome. Her existence gone from an intricate melody of bright, well-timed notes to a long-held, somber chord that carried over from measure to measure. One endless night after another supplied infinite hours to ruminate on the direction of her future without a break even to catch her breath. It was long past time to admit she'd gotten stuck in an endless contemplative rut and was no closer to understanding the ideal direction for her future. She might just have to take the plunge, get moving again and see where she ended up.

Crap. Relying on fate had never been her strong suit.

She cringed at an ultra-loud creak that shattered the still air. It came from a plank tucked beneath the Persian runner. Funny how the noisy floorboards had seemed charming when Aunt Rose inhabited the house. Now, they verged on creepy. Maybe she could find someone to fix the loose wood.

Logan, her mind whispered. She promptly ignored the ridiculous excuse to call him, talk to him or, God forbid, see him. If she'd resisted, though barely, his sexy rasp spicing up her voicemail on the day of Aunt Rose's funeral, she certainly wasn't about to cave to silly girlish whims now. Still, it might be time to make this place her own. Or move on.

The prospect of shopping for new furnishings began to perk her up. Hooray for the internet, an insomniac's playground. A mental list coalesced. She ticked off places to browse and what she'd need from each as she headed toward her room, seeking the laptop perched on her side table. The screensaver's abstract shapes transformed into others, glowing with colors that lured her closer like a moth to a retail flame. No reason not to get a jump on things. She had saved a folder of inspiration pictures on one of the home decorating sites she liked to idle away time on while dreaming about...*someday*.

Tomorrow could be someday.

Well, more like today since midnight had drifted past hours ago.

Enough of this stagnation.

Simply because she didn't need to work to survive given the insurance settlement from her parents' deaths, the generosity of Aunt Rose and the success of her previous career, didn't mean she had to idle all her time away. Committed to progress, even something as small as new curtains, she marched deeper into her sanctuary.

From the quaint lavender room Aunt Rose had tried to get her to abandon for a larger space, a flicker of light across the yard caught her attention. Next door, Rose's lifelong friend still occupied his similar home. Built within a month of each other, the two houses had hosted their owners for damn near fifty years, if not more.

There were times Kyana had to catch herself from thinking of her great aunt's neighbor as *Uncle* Ben. Maybe he was having trouble sleeping again too. It wouldn't be the first time she'd spied his bedside lamp shining like a beacon at all hours of the night since she'd returned home to care for her ailing relative. Some of her partners couldn't understand what they'd called a major sacrifice, but it had been the least she could do considering how Rose had taken her in all those years ago, after the accident that had stolen her parents from them.

Honestly, she regretted staying away as long as she had.

Kyana had learned to switch her own light off to keep from worrying Benjamin. At his age, he didn't need any more stress. Certainly not over her. She could handle herself—or so she'd always thought.

She squinted at the flicker, surprised to see it coming from the kitchen instead of the upstairs as she'd first assumed. Unsteady, the spark began to writhe and grow. Her eyes bulged as she pressed her nose to the glass. A tendril of gray smoke seeped from the windows Benjamin insisted on cracking open at night despite the air-conditioning he'd had installed decades ago and her concerns about security.

A fire!

Kyana snatched her cell phone off her nightstand and dialed 911 before she made it to the landing halfway down the stairs. The operator remained infuriatingly calm as Kyana shouted the address and crucial information at the well-intentioned woman. "Please, come quickly. Ben's bedroom is right above the kitchen."

"Ma'am, I've dispatched the firemen. Please stand back from the scene. You don't want to interfere. You'll be in their way."

She held the phone away from her face and gave it an oh-*hell*-no glare before disconnecting. In their speck of an upstate New York town, the firemen were all volunteers. They had to be roused from warm beds before driving in from who-knows-where. Not a chance in hell she'd let Benjamin sleep in a burning house. Without his hearing aids in, he might not notice the screeching detectors. Hell, half the time the cantankerous guy yanked the batteries from the devices after scorching his toast and left the housings dangling like open clamshells until she noticed and reassembled them.

Wet grass squished between her toes, soggy from the late spring showers they'd had almost every day for weeks. Sprinting across the lawn that divided Aunt Rose and Benjamin's houses, she hoped the dampness would impede the blaze.

As she neared, flares of light and heat billowed from the kitchen window, causing her to stumble backward with a gasp. Losing her footing, she ruined her favorite chemise with an ass-shaped splotch of mud. Pain shot up her tailbone and elbow, which took the brunt of the crash.

Acrid smoke scorched her lungs when she recovered from having the wind knocked out of her. She didn't dare pause to catch her breath. The edge of her nightgown passed as a filter when she yanked it over her mouth and scrambled to her feet. She raced up the porch stairs two at a time, palming the key from above the side entryway in half a second flat. Her hands shook. Metal slipped against slightly warmer than usual metal. At least she didn't drop the damn thing. On the second try, it notched into lock.

She moved the fabric protecting her face aside long enough to yell, "Ben! Wake up! Fire!"

The next breath she took contained enough smoke to have her choking as she finally crashed through the door. The lovely carved maple hit the entryway wall hard enough to leave a mark, but she didn't pause. No way could she dash through the kitchen without becoming a human shish kebab. Thank God the house had a second, if narrow, set of stairs in the rear.

"Ben!"

Kyana made as much noise as possible. Shouts dwindled in her narrowing windpipe. Fumes thickened as she ascended. They turned her cries scratchy. Coughing replaced most of her calls, so she preserved her oxygen.

She opened Ben's door cautiously, relieved to find the insidious conflagration hadn't yet eaten through the floor. However, her eyes watered beneath the assault of dense smoke. Tears streamed down her cheeks when she caught sight of an unmoving lump beneath the fugly harvest gold and green paisley quilt straight out of the seventies. It seemed too small to contain all the laugher and vitality she associated with Ben.

Please, please, don't be too late.

Shaking him didn't seem to help any more than screaming her brains out had. Something downstairs gave a horrible wail then a pop. Silence was followed by the *whoosh* of rejuvenated flames. Kyana couldn't believe how fast the fire had engulfed the lower level.

Neither she nor Ben had time to waste.

Uncertain of where she found the strength, she ducked down and tried to imitate the fireman's hold she'd seen on TV. Ben toppled to the floor, taking her balance with him. She crashed to the ground, smacking her head and shoulder on the corner of a dresser nearby. Stars danced in her vision, lulling her, tempting her to close her eyes for just one second.

No! Ben!

Staying low to the ground this time, she crawled over the unconscious man and used the cotton of his T-shirt at his shoulders to drag him toward the stairs. Thank God he'd never covered his precious hardwood floors. The polished surface made him easy to slide as she backed up to the landing. Glancing over her shoulder, she caught claws of fire rending the edges of the wall at the bottom of the stairs. She had no choice but to try and make it past before they blocked the entryway.

Sweat poured down her face, neck and back. Not all of it from the heat. Quivering, her muscles strained to obey her commands.

The door to the outside stood open. In the distance, she thought she heard the faint whine of a siren. So close. If she could just make it a little further, they'd be okay. Someone would be waiting outside to help. She hoped.

Kyana gave in to the very rare temptation to pray. She begged Aunt Rose to watch over them. To let there be something the experts could do to wake Ben up. Allowing herself to think it might be a corpse she hauled wasn't productive. She refused to believe that was true.

"Gonna be a rough ride. Hang on." She lifted his head and shoulders as high as she could without going ass over tea kettle then scooted down the stairs. If every single lungful hadn't seared her from the inside out, she might have winced at the thud of his heels banging on each riser they passed.

Overexertion, or maybe the knock she'd taken on her skull, stole her coordination. She screeched as she slipped, trying futilely to hang on to Ben as she tumbled down the last four or five steps. Landing in a heap at the bottom, she struggled to sort out their limbs. Until a wash of angry fire licked her side.

Instinct engaged. With one final burst of strength, she latched onto Ben's arm and hauled him across the threshold onto the low deck outside. "Have to get away. Further from the house."

Kyana didn't realize she chanted the mantra as she repeatedly blinked her eyes to clear the haze and infuse some moisture to the dry, tortured surfaces.

"It's okay, miss." Someone pried her fingers from Ben. "I have you."

"Ben!"

"Your friend's safe. Thanks to you. Come on. We'll get you both sorted out." The world tipped and turned. She couldn't bring herself to care or to decipher the surreal sensation of being carried for the first time she could ever remember. "Christ, you're a brave one. Running into that mess is enough to scare our rookies over there."

"No choice." She let her head rest on the black and neon striped surface of the fireman's jacket. Even those two tiny words ripped up her throat.

"Shush." He rocked her as he broke into a jog. "You could have actually listened to the dispatcher and not charged into that fucker yourself. But I would've done exactly the same thing. Get used to being called a hero, honey. The news crew is eating this shit up. By tomorrow morning, you're going to be famous. At least around here."

Flashing red lights intensified until they nearly blinded her, given her already impaired vision. The fireman deposited her gently on a gurney. He squeezed her fingers then disappeared, diving right into the hell she'd been so eager to flee.

Medics swarmed her.

"Ben." The emphatic shout sounded more like a rasp.

"He's breathing," a woman informed her. "A good sign. Let my partners do their jobs. How about not making mine any harder by fighting, huh? Settle down."

Gentle touches accompanied the stern request. A mask fell into place over her mouth. Cool air soothed her throat and lungs.

"Inhale. Slow and deep." The woman's dulcet voice charmed Kyana, forcing her to obey for several long minutes while the shock and terror of what had happened began to really sink in. She subdued the urge to rotate for a glimpse of Ben, afraid of what she might witness.

A growl rumbled through the night. "Let me up. Take that crap off me."

"Ben." Kyana smiled.

"I see the two of you are a matched set." The EMT rolled her eyes. "Your dad is going to be just fine."

"He's not—" She stopped herself. In some ways he kind of had been. For both her and his great-nephew, Logan. A vision of the rogue bad boy next door inspired Kyana's insides to cartwheel just as surely as he had during the summer and final year of high school they'd spent as neighbors and friends.

His dark, unruly hair and bright blue eyes were a potent combination she'd never forget. Not even a decade-long parade of handsome actors, who starred in the romantic comedies she adored, had offered up daydream material half as fine.

Unfortunately, she'd never appealed to Logan in the same way. She refused to think of the time she'd begged him to kiss her, right here beneath the sprawling oak tree in the yard that separated their houses. An instant or ten of heaven followed by several weeks of awkward purgatory that'd ended when he took off a few days before graduation.

She'd never even said goodbye.

"Your eyes will probably be watering for days." The woman patted her shoulder. "That's totally normal considering how much smoke you were exposed to."

If only that were the cause. Much easier to treat than an unrequited yet everlasting crush on your ridiculous first...*only*...love.

"Kyana?" Ben's voice took on a new level of alarm. "She *what*? Where is she?"

Rather than risk him injuring himself further, Kyana waved off her tech and slithered to the ground. She stripped the mask from her face, and ignored the vehement protests of most of her body, including her hip, which was visible through the charred hole in her nightgown.

"Right here," she croaked. So much for reassuring him. "Just fine."

"Oh, girly." Ben slumped in his makeshift bed. "You look like shit."

"Gee, thanks." She grinned.

He opened his arms, and she didn't pause before throwing herself into his still-strong grasp. "You're shaking. It's alright now, Ky. At least until I beat your ass for putting yourself in danger like that."

She tried to stop the tears from falling, but couldn't. "I thought I was too late."

"I'm tougher than you think." He ruffled her hair.

"Ms. Brady! Mr. Patterson!" Kyana lifted her face from Ben's shoulder instinctively. The second she faced the intrusion, bright lights gleamed, shocking her already sore eyes. She squinted, trying to make out the person on the other side of the glare. "This is Channel Four news. How did the fire start? Is there anyone else in the house?"

Kyana stammered some half-answer, trying to make it stop. The noise, the light, the endless barrage of questions—it was all too much for her battered senses.

"Enough." A tall man, dressed in dark clothing, emerged from the shadows to issue the grim command. His upright bearing and the panther-like stalk to his approach clearly identified him as Daryl Thick.

Kyana couldn't recall hearing much more than one word sentences from the ex-military man in all the time he'd lived down the street. To be honest, he'd kind of freaked her out with his stillness and the intensity of his stare on more than one occasion. Like tonight, he always seemed to be lurking in the shadows.

Watching.

Waiting.

For what, she wasn't sure, but she sure appreciated the effortless way he squashed the newsman's inquisition tonight. "I've got this, Ben. No more questions folks. Move along."

Ben lifted his hand, but Daryl had already run the reporter behind the police line. His imposing form and the stubborn set of his enormous shoulders brooked no argument.

Kyana's gaze roamed from the clash to the rest of the people huddled on the sidewalk. She couldn't recognize all of their neighbors from this distance, despite the orange glow cast by the flames. At the front of the pack was the young couple who'd moved in less than a year ago. She returned their solemn wave. They looked as miserable as she felt, huddled together, horrified.

She had to look away from the pity in their stares before she allowed herself to consider all that Ben had lost. In a matter of minutes, a lifetime of possessions, photographs, and memories had been destroyed.

A sob escaped her chest.

"I'm sorry," she gasped. "There wasn't time to grab anything."

"You hauled my wrinkled old ass out of there, girly." Ben ruffled her hair. "Nothing else matters.

I've got all the important stuff up here. And in here."

She smiled softly when he tapped his temple then his chest with a gnarled finger.

"Benjamin!" A wail cut through the din of the fire, which seemed to be lessening beneath the onslaught of water and the firemen crawling over Ben's house like florescent ants. Barked directions, the squeal of additional sirens approaching and the rumble of the gathering crowd had nothing on the high-pitched screech that emanated from the tiny elderly woman tottering their way.

"Incoming," Ben muttered.

Kyana couldn't help but laugh. Her aunt and Ben had often resorted to all sorts of hijinks in order to dodge their clingy, busybody neighbor through the years.

Why should Myrtle's overdramatic bent lean a different direction tonight? At least she would have plenty to gossip about for the next few weeks.

"Be nice. Let her fuss over you. It'll make her feel useful." Kyana patted Ben's shoulder.

Nothing beat seeing her seventy-two year old neighbor rolling his eyes a moment before Myrtle descended on them with gasps, cries and hugs for Ben. For the first time since she'd spotted the wisp of fire from her bedroom window, Kyana felt like things might be okay.

Eventually.

CHAPTER TWO

Logan crashed onto the beat-up leather recliner in his shitty apartment. Sure, it was barely after dawn, but it wasn't early by his standards. Usually he raced the first rays of sunrise to a construction site. This morning was really the end of a long, long night and a terrible day.

His buzz had faded hours ago, somewhere around the time he'd realized he couldn't get it up with the slightly skanky blonde who'd promised to suck all his woes right out of him in some even sketchier alley. Probably the one behind the bar he'd attempted to drown his sorrows in. What the hell was wrong with him?

It wasn't every day a guy got canned, he supposed.

Not that he hadn't seen that train barreling down on him from a mile away. Still, he'd tried his damnedest to save his spot on the renovation crew by working his ass off. Demonstrating superior skills and reliability hadn't been the Hail Mary he'd hoped. Hell, he'd even skipped out on Rose's funeral so he wouldn't have to call off. What a waste. He'd left a pathetic message on

Kyana's voicemail, offering condolences he should have given in person. No wonder she hadn't called his lame ass back.

Not now or ten years ago when he'd walked out on her and Ben like the chickenshit eighteen-year-old he'd been.

It was about time he got his priorities in order. As soon as he could believe this had really happened. Grief, fury and shock sweated from his skin along with the vile stench left behind by a 40 of King Cobra—the most buzz he could buy for his last twenty, drinking like a hobo. Might as well have duct-taped the bottle to his palm. At least then he wouldn't have knocked it over, spilling some. He really could have used those last six or seven shots. Maybe they would have granted him oblivion.

Logan tipped his head onto the comfortable cushion, which had dented to perfectly contour his form years ago. He tried not to think of the shit he'd lost in his life, like the gorgeous young lady he'd admired and wanted so desperately. Her delicate Asian features, refined manners, unwavering loyalty to her mongrel best friend, and her all-American sass had practically brought him to his knees. Just another thing he'd never really had a chance at holding on to.

What a loser.

Doubly so because the simple thought of her—and the sultry all-woman voice that had transfixed him on her voicemail—had blood rushing to his dick. If it had been her smooshed up against him in that cesspool tonight, there'd have been no performance issues to stand in the way of a mind-numbing good time. Yeah, right. Kyana would never stoop so low as to join him in a dive like that. He didn't blame her either.

"Son of a bitch!" He thumped his fist on the tattered arm of his chair, refusing to give in to the temptation to take matters into his own hands while visions of the polished, perfect girl next door danced through his mind. He'd grown out of that phase back in high school. Okay, he had occasional relapses, but it hadn't been until Ben told Logan she'd moved home during one of their twice weekly calls that he'd regressed to his former obsession.

Ben would be awake in an hour or so. Maybe Logan would call and see what was going on in the old neighborhood. He'd crash-landed there when his mom hooked up with a new guy and didn't have room or patience to take a rebellious teen along to her new picket-fence life. He didn't really blame her.

Better yet, maybe he should pay his great uncle a visit. It was about time Logan did something useful. Something decent for someone who deserved his loyalty.

He still couldn't believe he'd been played so bad. A total sucker. How hadn't he realized what was up?

To distract himself for a while, he snatched the remote off the side table, which he'd rescued on junk day and restored, before flipping on the

TV. Channel surfing his basic cable didn't yield much of interest.

Infomercial, infomercial, infomercial…

News.

It might do him some good to remember there were entire nations of people out there who had it a hell of a lot worse than he did. Fucked up? Yes. But it did make him feel better about the state of his existence. If he could find an old Jerry Springer rerun he'd really be looking fine.

Flames transfixed him as they wrapped around the edges of a window to grasp at the shutter outside. Wow, it would seriously blow to have your pad burn down. Especially if you had a home instead of merely a place you stayed, which is how he felt lately. The fire hypnotized him as it licked at the walls of an older Victorian that looked not that different than the one he'd spent his adolescent summers in. Ben's house had been home. The real kind. For a while.

Maybe Logan could try for that again.

He leaned forward in his chair as a fireman burst from the rear of the building with a woman cradled in his arms. Raven hair and pale skin wrapped in something that might once have been pretty blue silk were revealed with each cycle of the flashing emergency lights.

Logan's head tilted as he examined the injured woman. He must have been more fucked up than he realized to imagine the damsel in distress looked a hell of a lot like Kyana. Not that he'd studied her photographs in Ben and Rose's houses on his infrequent visits or anything.

Sure, sure. Keep telling yourself those lies. One day you might believe them, buddy.

Shit, he'd even snapped his own copies with his cell phone. The woman he'd spied in designer suits or in endless graduation cap and gowns on Rose's vintage mantle didn't seem like the sort who'd doll herself up in gorgeous yet frivolous finery. He scrubbed his eyes with the bruised and cut knuckles of one hand when he realized he hadn't blinked for a sold thirty seconds.

When he refocused, he saw it—the ugly ass birdbath he and Kyana had built Ben one sweltering August afternoon as kids when her family had been on a round-the-world tour and his mom had been on the prowl for a step up. The broken flower pots they'd recycled made unlevel, garish yard art better suited to Logan's mom's trailer park than Ben's neat and trim community. Despite that, his great uncle had refused to get rid of the junk.

No! It can't be. He stabbed the volume button on his remote, disengaging the mute feature.

"The cause of the fire is still unknown but the resident was the only occupant at the time of the blaze. His neighbor spotted the fire, called emergency crews, then rushed inside to haul the elderly man from the flames." In the background, a burly fireman toted Kyana's rag doll form as though she weighed nothing at all. Tall and willowy, she probably didn't. The graininess of the image made it hard to tell much, but the tattered nightgown and soot stains covering her sent ice through Logan's veins.

"Neighbors tell us this isn't the first tragedy to strike Oak Avenue this year. The death of a longtime resident next door just a few months ago has some wondering if bad luck really does come in threes. And, if so, who will suffer it next?" The reporter paused while footage cut away from Kyana being loaded onto a gurney outside an ambulance.

"Go back! Go back!" He shouted at the TV. He had to make sure she was okay. And where was Ben? They'd said Ky had pulled him from the burning house, but was he all right?

Batty as ever, Myrtle Jansen entertained the reporter with old wives' tales and superstitions that portended more dire times to come. Logan shook his head and instead studied the rest of the crowd. He didn't recognize the man and woman huddled together in the background. They must be new to the area. Daryl Thick loomed still and watchful on the fringes of the frame. His assessing stare on Myrtle and the newscaster put Logan on instant alert.

"More on this story as it becomes available. Back to you, Tom…"

"What? That's it?" Logan didn't know when he'd launched to his feet but he paced the kitchen as he dug his cell from the back pocket of his jeans. He snagged his keys out of the bowl by the door as he jogged from his apartment.

Ring after ring grated on his nerves until he realized, of course, there'd be no answer at Ben's place. He used his thumb to search the contact list of his basic, un-smart phone for the number he'd only found the balls to dial once. After Rose's funeral. Kyana.

Instead of infuriating chimes, a beeping busy signal greeted him. "Damn it!"

He punched the steering wheel then jammed a key in the ignition of his pickup truck. At least there wouldn't be traffic at this time of day, and he'd gotten gas just a day or two ago. If he pushed it, he could make the drive in an hour.

It was the longest fifty-three minutes of his life.

Logan skidded to a halt in the driveway of Rose's house. No, Kyana's house. The yellow tape blocking off the entrance to Ben's place was completely unnecessary. Stopping there would have been pointless. Char lingered in the air, making his eyes water and his nose itch. He didn't pause to swipe at his face before tearing from the truck. He hopped the flower beds and retaining wall with a single leap before sprinting up the hill to the back stairs he'd used many times in his youth.

The bottom one creaked louder than he remembered, but maybe he'd never subjected it to such force in the past. Today he leapt them three at a time. He swiped the key from its usual hiding place in the grill, tucked in the corner of the deck, then burst through the screened-in porch. Without bothering to ring the bell, he let himself inside.

Lights blazed in the kitchen, so he headed that way first.

Logan was a little surprised to find his uncle awake after all the commotion, which had probably included a trip to the hospital in the handful of hours between the fire and the airing of the piece on the news. His heart stuttered in his chest when he caught sight of Ben, slumped over the dining room table. For the first time Logan could remember, the man looked...old. White hair slicked back from a recent shower. Neat rows left by a comb in his thinning locks contrasted with a fuzzy grey robe, which Ben clasped tight around him. It had obviously belonged to Rose. If Logan wasn't concentrating so hard on not breaking down, he might have snapped a picture.

"Nice outfit." He tried not to startle his great uncle. The guy didn't need that kind of shock on top of everything else.

"Even without my hearing aids, I could tell that was you clomping up the stairs. Maybe because you were shaking the whole damn house, you big lug." Ben lifted his head and pasted on a wry smile. "How'd you find out?"

"The goddamned news." He tried not to shout, balling his fists at his sides instead. He didn't bother with inane questions like, 'How are you?' when the answer was clearly devastated-yet-mostly-healthy. Besides, they were both more comfortable with confrontation than sentimental shit. "Were you going to call me? Or am I so worthless you didn't think I'd come?"

"Logan, please." Ben shook his head, his eyes shining. "Things have been rough lately, I understand. How many decades did I work two or three jobs to earn my house? When you have a dream, you have to go for it. Things—*important* things—have to be sacrificed. I wasn't about to pile any more pressure on you. We'll handle it."

"You and Wonder Woman, huh? I can't fucking believe she ran into a burning building." His guts roiled again at the thought of what might have happened. The ragdoll flop of her lithe body in the fireman's arms had him brewing some punches. Aimed at whom, he couldn't say. Maybe the dude who had been there to rescue her. Logan wished he could have been her hero.

The nightmare vision distracted him from pursuing Ben's revelation. What had the man sacrificed? Logan would give his great-uncle anything in his power. Another time he would circle around and find out.

"I'm torn on that one. Can't say I'm pleased she put herself at risk. At the same time... I'm sure I wouldn't be sitting here right now if it weren't for that girly." Ben sighed. "She's tough. You know she is. But a person can only take so much. She's been in the shower an awfully long time. I'm starting to think someone needs to make sure she's okay. I should have insisted the doctors examine her too, damn it. You know how she gets, though. Hardheaded."

Ben stared at Logan, unblinking.

"I'm on it." Logan bent down and clapped a hand on Ben's back, surprised to find his palm met with more bone than muscle. He manned up and said what he was really thinking all along. "I'm so glad you're all right."

"Me too, kiddo." Ben coughed when he laughed. "Guess I gotta go to extremes to rate a visit, huh?"

"Not anymore. I swear. Things'll be different. Shit, you might not be able to get rid of me now." Logan never broke promises. For one thing, his landlord was likely to boot him into the skid row gutter a millisecond after the dirt bag found out he'd lost his job. But mostly, being here felt right.

Though his world had turned upside down, something in his soul had settled the moment he'd driven his truck onto Oak Avenue—even if he'd executed the maneuver practically on two wheels.

Ben nodded then shooed Logan with a wave of his hands toward the stairs. "Check on, Kyana. I'm going to rest for a while. Is it sleep or a nap if it's already six o'clock? In either case, I'll take Rose's room."

They both winced at the reminder of their absent friend.

Overflowing with terror, loss and regret, Logan bounded up the stairs to the second floor.

He strode to the bathroom that adjoined Kyana's old room and banged on the door.

No answer.

She'd have to be deafer than Ben to miss his second round of pounding.

Still not a peep confronted his battery against the hardwood.

Something told him he'd have better luck convincing her to open the door if he didn't start bellowing at her from the other side of the six-paneled maple. If she recognized his voice, he'd certainly be left out in the cold.

Then he imagined her passed out. Unconscious. What if she'd slipped and hit her head?

She had to be exhausted.

Drained.

Scared.

Hurt.

It didn't take much for him to visualize her crumpled in the tile basin, bleeding from a nasty dent in her thick skull. Screw that.

He pivoted on one heel and marched into Rose's room. Ben looked at him with a single raised brow when he rummaged through the supplies near the vanity mirror. He held a bobby pin up to the soft morning light, glowing in the window, to judge the wire's gauge.

"You can't just barge in there. Give her space if she needs it," Ben protested, leaning forward from the edge of the bed. His fingers gripped Logan's arm hard enough to leave marks.

"She's not answering. What if she's messed up?" He paused, respecting the opinion of his great uncle. The man had practically raised him. During the time in between stays, Logan had merely been surviving, not learning and growing like he had been in the glorious summers or the final year he'd spent on Oak Avenue.

"Shit, you're right." Ben closed his eyes. "No choice. Be ready for her to fight you though. She's a wildcat, our girly."

"I think I can handle one wet, naked woman." He groaned. It took all the fortitude he possessed to halt that line of fantasy right in its tracks. "Damn. I didn't mean it like that…"

Ben laughed. "I didn't raise a dumbass. She's likely to tear your nuts off as it is. Good luck, son."

Logan grimaced and adjusted his package as he made his way to the bathroom door. He tried once more, rapping in a more reasonable tone. One deep breath. Two. Three.

He gritted his teeth and got to work finessing the lock. It took him less than five seconds to disengage it even with the crude bobby pin. Some habits die hard.

Yeah, like lusting after Kyana Brady. Somehow he figured what he was about to do wouldn't simplify that situation.

Logan paused with his shaking fingers on the knob. He sighed then turned the antique glass and porcelain handle. Steam billowed from the crack when he pushed the door open, making him wonder how Kyana had managed to maneuver through the smoke in Ben's house. She must have been terrified, but she hadn't let that stop her from saving his great uncle's life.

He owed her one. A monstrously huge one.

"Kyana?" he called out as he inched forward, shutting the door gently behind him. "Are you all right?"

Waving his arms in front of him, he advanced through the cloud of lightly scented mist. It smelled of something exotic. Jasmine and green tea, which reminded him of Kyana's half-Japanese heritage. He'd always adored her long, black hair and the gorgeous shape of her unusual hazel eyes.

A tiny hiccup yanked him from the memory of her smile.

"Ky?" He tilted his head to make sense of the jumble of limbs curled into a tight ball on the shower floor. For a moment he thought he'd had it right. She must have slipped and fallen. Who knew how long she'd lain there suffering. "Oh, fuck."

Without hesitation, he tugged open the clear glass enclosure and sank to his knees beside her. The door banged a little as it swung closed. The noise startled Kyana. If he hadn't already reached for her, she might have slammed into the wall in her haste to retreat. Instead, he caged her against his chest, giving no thought to his rapidly dampening clothes.

"Where are you hurt?" Warm spray blasted his back. Nothing could have burned as bright as the woman he held in his arms. Even if she was trying her damnedest to break free.

Logan didn't plan to let her go any time soon.

"*What?* I'm not. I'm fine. What the hell—?" She thrashed for a few seconds more, until his gentle rambling broke through her initial fear.

"It's me. Logan. I've got you. Everything's going to be okay. I'm sorry I frightened you. I tried to knock. You didn't respond. I thought you might need me. I was afraid. It killed me to see you lying there. Let me help. Let me help."

She went limp in his arms. So much so, he might have thought she'd fainted for real except the momentary relaxation didn't last. A shuddering sob ripped through her. All resistance fled. Like a pendulum that'd reached one extreme, she swung the other way. Latching on to him, she crawled so close on his lap he might have thought she'd burrowed inside his jeans if they hadn't stuck to him like a second skin.

"It's really you. You're here." She explored the tops of his arms, ringing as much of his biceps as she could with her long, delicate fingers. Apparently satisfied, she gulped then buried her face in his neck.

Sheltering her gave him a purpose, and made him feel a million feet tall.

He didn't pause to protect her modesty. Bold strokes of his hands were designed to infuse her with warmth and strength. He hugged her to him until she squeaked through her soul-deep cries. Somehow, he suspected this could be the first time she'd let her guard drop completely since Rose's death. Hell, maybe ever.

Rocking them both, he allowed his own tears to fall unnoticed. A couple for his job. More for the fear that had chilled his heart this morning. And a torrent for the amazing woman all three of them had loved and lost. But most for the time he'd wasted. Because holding Kyana now he realized… This was home. The place he'd always been destined to be happiest.

Maybe not right this second. Still, together they could endure anything. They had in the past and they would again if he had anything to say about it.

Little by little, her crying diminished. Sniffles and plaintive whimpers ripped his insides apart faster than the violent heaving of her sobs had. Goosebumps rose on her skin when the water began to cool. "Come on, Kyana-chan."

A delicate snort interrupted her mourning. "I haven't heard that one in a while."

Logan separated them only enough to peer into her bloodshot-yet-beautiful eyes. "Get used to it. I have a feeling you'll be sick of it before long."

"Never." She bit her lip as if to keep it from trembling. Had she ever looked so vulnerable? He doubted it. The usual armor she buckled around herself had vanished along with her clothes. "I missed you, Logan-kun. I'm glad you're here."

"Same goes."

The silence lingered forever between them. He'd never longed to kiss a woman as badly as he did in that instant. Her tongue darted around to soothe her chapped lips and he almost stroked out. For the first time, he allowed his gaze to wander from her face. But instead of sneaking a peak at her high, firm breasts, he caught sight of several massive bruises.

Arms, ribs, hips—the perfection of her body was marred by ghastly purple splotches.

"You *are* hurt." He rose to his feet, ensuring his grip on her elbows lifted her as well. He ducked his shoulder to press in the handle and shut the water off.

"I don't feel it when I'm with you." She smiled up at him. The resulting riot of butterflies in his chest almost distracted him enough to carry her straight to bed.

"Like hell." He set her carefully on the countertop, subduing her shriek on contact. The cooler marble chilled her still steaming, extra-fine ass. Inspecting her bruises and cuts, he determined only a few needed bandages. The worst of the damage seemed to be the singed patch on her hip.

"They gave me some ointment for that." She pointed toward a pile of supplies he hadn't noticed in his haste to reach her. "If you hand it to me—"

"Shush." He covered her lips with his fingers. Sure, it kept her quiet. Better yet, it stopped him from doing something foolish. Like closing the gap between them to press his mouth to hers. That wasn't the kind of comfort she would appreciate from him. She deserved way better than an uneducated, unemployed twenty-eight-year-old bum.

Without glancing away from her, he retrieved the tube of cream and the loose gauze paired with it. He concentrated on applying a generous layer to her ultra-soft skin without inflicting any more pain. That was the last thing he aimed to do.

No matter how hard he tried to ignore her svelte curves or the long lines of her torso and legs, it was no use. Even more attractive was her self-confidence. Not once did she try to cross her arms over her breasts or arrange a towel on top of her lap. If she could be adult about her nudity, so could he. Mostly. Probably.

Wet, stifling jeans reduced the likelihood he'd succumb to baser instincts and ravage her on the vanity to about a fifteen percent chance. He figured he couldn't hope for better.

As if she read his mind, Kyana traced the shoulder seam of his saturated T-shirt. "You're still wearing your clothes. They must be cold. And weigh a ton."

"I'm fine," he grumbled as he lightly rubbed the last of the adhesive holding the bandage into place, allowing himself a few extra passes to be really sure it held, and to savor the softness of her skin. She shivered.

"You're sort of making mud puddles." She winced as she spied the bathmat that had been collateral damage in their skirmish.

"Oh, shit." He jerked. Count on him to ruin Kyana's pretty things. He whipped his shirt over his head, unbuckled his belt, stripped his jeans down his thighs and kicked off his boots in less time than it took her to reassure him it was no big deal. Placing his filthy shoes in the shower for cleanup later, he faced her once more.

Her jaw hung open.

"Damn. Sorry." He assessed the damage. "I think I can get that out. If not, I'll replace it. I promise."

"Huh?" She blinked.

Twice.

A slow, irrepressible smile wiped the dread from his mind when he realized she scoped him just as hard as he'd done to her. Except she was far less skilled in subtle appreciation. For once he was proud of the way his hard work had honed his body. From her, the attention felt like a mighty big compliment.

Kyana's chest rose and fell faster as her gaze swept down his torso, over the ink and his piercings to the pronounced bulge in his drenched briefs. The fabric felt like it'd shrunk in the shower, or maybe the constriction was thanks to the massive hard-on his fantasy girl inspired.

She swallowed hard, then choked.

"Thanks," he murmured as he took the opportunity to scoop her off the counter and lower her to the floor. The glide of their damp skin tortured them equally. "Same goes, by the way. You grew up really well, Ky."

"I— Damn. Sorry. I didn't mean to stare." Her pretty porcelain skin turned pink.

"I did." Logan snagged a plush towel off the rack and wrapped her in its softness. He buffed her arms and legs, making sure not to press any sore spots too hard, then wrapped a smaller cloth around her hair before attending to himself with a handful of swipes.

When he turned to put the towel in the hamper, Kyana plucked his clothes from the floor. She arranged his shirt over the shower door then dug in his jeans, rescuing his faux-leather wallet. He didn't stop her fast enough.

His face heated, glowing as red as an overheated saw blade when she removed his ID and the last three crumpled singles he had left to his name. Instead of laughing at his pathetic life savings, she flattened the trio of bills on the counter and propped the cheap pleather open to allow air to circulate through the barren folds.

She distracted him from his discomfort when she peeked up from beneath long, if not curled, lashes. The raw vulnerability he spied in her eyes made him feel a little more on even footing. "Logan..."

"Yeah?"

"Will you stay with me tonight?"

"I don't have anywhere else to go, Ky."

"You're welcome to stay as long as you need." She didn't pry, just nodded, though her shoulders seemed to slump a little. Avoiding looking at him, she scooted past, into her bedroom.

"Hey, wait. That didn't sound right." He scrubbed his hand through his hair, thinking of the countless fuck-ups he'd made when it came to her. All the times he'd said the wrong thing. Or had been too afraid to try to find the perfect thing.

No more of that bullshit. Time to man up.

Crossing the threshold to her sanctuary, he took a gamble. "It wouldn't matter. You know, if I had a hundred homes. This is where I want to be tonight. I'm only sorry I wasn't here earlier. You shouldn't have had to deal with this, all of it, on your own. It's been a long-ass time, but I'm still the same guy who was your friend. I haven't forgotten how you always had my back. Now let me get yours."

From a hand-glazed dresser, she withdrew a gossamer garment intended to drive men insane with lust and admiration. Mission accomplished when it fluttered into place around her ideal form, leaving a surprising string of pink, white and red cherry blossoms exposed on her shoulder. He wouldn't have expected her to go for tattoos, but the artwork suited her. It made his cock ten times harder.

"I've got things under control."

"I don't doubt that." He watched her slip beneath the lush duvet and ridiculously soft-looking sheets. "But you can lean on me tonight.

Today. Whatever the hell it is out there. And always. I hope you understand that."

He considered getting in bed with his underwear on but didn't want to risk the cheap black dye staining her fancy linens. With a shrug, he shimmied out of the sticky fabric, tossed it over his shoulder into the bathroom then strode to the bed.

Kyana's laser-beam stare tracked his every movement until he obscured her view with the duvet, staying on top of the sheet she rested under. He wasn't some kind of creeper who'd try to molest her when she was down...no matter how desperately the primal parts of his brain encouraged him to try.

They both lay on their backs, staring at the ceiling for a while. A chasm at least a foot wide separated their tense bodies in her luxurious bed. When he couldn't stand it another second, he slid his hand beneath her shoulders and tugged. "This is stupid. We're adults now. Come here."

Thankfully, she didn't fight. She laid her head on his shoulder and curled up to his side, with only the thin sheet separating them.

Logan decided it was time to go all or nothing. Lying wasn't his style any more these days than it had been in high school. Hiding his feelings then had almost killed him.

"Sweet dreams, Kyana-chan." He tipped up her chin and claimed her mouth in a brief kiss. Brushing his lips against hers, he relished her taste and the complete surrender she offered him.

Resisting the urge to plunder, he attempted to illustrate the tumble of emotions rolling around in his guts. Slow, tender and lingering contact seemed to do the trick.

When they parted, they both were breathless.

"Welcome home," she rasped.

Something inside of him stood up and cheered, knowing not all of the huskiness had to do with the smoke she'd inhaled. He linked their fingers on top of the covers and rubbed his thumb over her speeding pulse.

Despite the different worlds they came from and the string of tragedies that had hammered them lately, they both fell asleep with smiles on their faces.

CHAPTER THREE

Kyana stretched, groaning at the soreness permeating her muscles. Especially the ones around her mouth, which guaranteed she'd grinned like a rapper showing off diamond-studded grills all night long. Logan was home. He'd come on his own. And he'd kissed her like he meant it. At least it'd seemed as though he relished the reunion as much as she had.

Shaking her head, she silently swore she wouldn't mistake his inherent passion as desire aimed specifically at her. Not this time. Suddenly she felt seventeen again—clueless, unsure of herself, and bursting with hope despite the reality check her practical side attempted to administer.

She might have thought being swept off her feet by her lifetime crush was some delusional dream—maybe one caused by the pain medication she'd popped before stumbling into the shower last night—if it weren't for the smell of the man he'd grown into, which lingered on her sheets, or the dark scrap of his abandoned briefs on the cream marble tile of her bathroom floor. He certainly hadn't gotten any neater in his maturity. Though he had plenty of perks to offset that quirk.

Ho-ly crap. His wet, sculpted body had been sexier than every fantasy she'd had about him all rolled into one. Defined muscles, bold artwork and his filled-out form were far superior to the lean yet tough build of the teenager who'd convinced her to go skinny dipping once. And that had been a sight to behold. Still, the compassion in his gaze had trumped even his physical perfection in her esteem. As if he'd realized she needed him desperately, like she had when the wound of her parent's loss had been fresh and ugly, he'd appeared from nowhere, materializing out of the steam.

Then again, he'd disappeared just as stealthily. Both the eve of their high school graduation and today, when he'd tiptoed from her room with the grace of a jungle cat. Kyana hadn't roused herself fast enough from the first totally peaceful sleep she'd managed since her Aunt Rose's funeral—probably months before then, really—to stop him.

Maybe he'd ridden an adrenaline high after discovering their near miss. Though she'd wrangled her first choice of companions by some miracle, he could have needed someone, *anyone*, to cling to in an attempt to keep the horror of what might have been at bay. She wouldn't blame him in the least for that. Smiling as she drew on a robe, she hoped she'd conjured half as much solace for him as he'd granted her.

The smell of citrus, and something else she couldn't quite put her finger on, lured her toward the kitchen despite the awkward situation awaiting her at the end of the stairs. Salivation kicked in, though her drooling problem had more to do with the shirtless man cooking as skillfully as Hubert Keller than the salmon filets she spotted searing in the copper pan he wielded as if he were as familiar with it as his favorite hammer.

Rose's favorite floral hand towel was tucked in Logan's waistband. Kyana had never envied a scrap of terrycloth before. The slight singe mark on the corner had her shaking her head as she remembered the day Myrtle Jansen had accidentally scorched the fabric while heating up some food Rose didn't have the appetite for. They should have tossed the rag in the garbage after Kyana had discovered it smoking beside the mac and cheese in the oven. No one had. Logan ran his fingers down the fabric as if drawing some of Rose's legendary strength from the scrap.

"Too bad, Ben." He shook his head and continued without turning around. "You can't send me away. I'm not going. Not this time."

"You're always welcome, Logan. Don't make it sound like I'm giving you the boot. But I won't have you risking that job of yours. You love it. In fact, you'd best hit the road soon if you're going to be rested enough for those early morning shifts you pull."

"There's nothing to go back to." He dropped the pan on the cooktop with a final clank. "That's what I'm trying to say. Badly. I'm fucked, Ben. I lost everything. I got fired."

"How?" Kyana burst into the room, hands on hips. "I've seen pictures of your work. You're amazing at what you do. This is bullshit."

"Ky." He whipped around. "Damn. I guess there's no hiding anything around here anyway."

"What happened, son?" Ben motioned for Logan to join him at the table, but their impromptu chef didn't do anything half-assed. He concentrated on situating a divine hunk of salmon on each of the three plates he'd garnished with lemon wedges and something green. Where the hell had he scrounged that stuff from?

"Nicholson cut corners. Used cheap material that wouldn't hold up. The bastard asked me to cover for the company. No fucking way. I fixed a few of the issues on my own, couldn't stand to see the homeowners get screwed like that. But I ran out of money fast. So the next time it happened, I told the inspector about the violations myself." His shoulders slumped as he wiped his hands on a dish towel. "The foreman no longer required my services after that."

"This really is crap." Injustice spurred Kyana to don her lawyer hat for the first time in months. "We can fight this."

"And then what?" He shook his head as he approached with a steaming plate balanced on his sculpted forearm and two more laid out on his palms. "I go back to work for a dickhead who has it out for me? Or I'm owed a boatload of cash he doesn't have unless he rips off more unsuspecting homeowners? It's not worth it."

Ben shook his head. "One thing at a time. Help me fix my house. Those outrageous premiums I've shelled out for an eternity should mean insurance can afford what you deserve to make for the job you'll do. This could be the break you need to get your own business off the ground. A portfolio builder."

"If the payout is short or slow, I'll kick in the supplies as long as you provide the labor." Kyana played with the artful arrangement on the plate Logan handed her without meeting his gaze. She knew how touchy he could be about something that meant nothing to her. Money had always been a sticking point between them, no matter how delicately she tread. "Rose would have loved to help you. Hell, she would have insisted."

"Absolutely not." Logan's objection didn't surprise her. "I'm not taking any handouts."

Ben snorted. "This ain't some kind of charity, kid. No one's offering you something for nothing. Your job isn't going to be easy. I'm a damn picky customer. Especially when it comes to my house."

"Ben needs someone he can trust. You wouldn't leave him in the hands of a scammer like your piece of shit boss would you? And being a partner in a startup could be just the project I've been looking for. I can help you with all the legal and management junk." Kyana rushed to bolster Ben's argument when he peered up at her with wide blue eyes.

"I couldn't—"

"You will. You, me and our girly. It'll be like the good old times. When we were a family. She's right, you know. Rose would insist if she were here. So don't argue with your elders." Ben glared.

"Ky's younger than me." Logan pouted.

How could he manage that and still be so damn sexy?

"By three weeks!" She winged a steamed green bean at his smirk, both annoyed and impressed when he caught it out of mid-air then popped it between his bright white teeth. *Mmm.*

"Fine. You can bicker with her all you like. After we eat." Ben rapped Logan's powerful thigh with the back of his hand. "Give me that dish. Let's dig in before this gets cold."

Logan opened his mouth then closed it again, respecting his uncle's wishes. He set a plate in front of Ben, and sank into one of the ornate chairs Rose had hunted from an antique sale. The stately furniture looked like it belonged in a dollhouse when he graced it.

"Good morning to you too, Ojii-san." Kyana kissed Ben's temple lightly then claimed the chair he and Logan drew out for her simultaneously. Sandwiched between them, she felt safe...and hungry. How long had it been since she'd really had an appetite?

"Same to you." He winked. "More like good evening. Logan was going to bring you dinner in bed. Hurry up and scoot under the covers if you want, I won't tell him you're awake. Maybe he hasn't noticed."

"I sure as hell picked up on that, but it wouldn't stop me from making a special delivery." He licked a daub of cream sauce from his fork. The sensuality he harnessed even in such a small gesture gave her heart palpitations.

She cleared her throat before trying to play it cool. "I'm not about to make him serve me after he already did all the work."

"It would be my pleasure." The heat in his stare scorched her twice over yet somehow it gave her shivers too. "You'd better get used to it. If I'm going to be staying here, I'll be pulling my weight."

"I vote for him as our cook." Ben forked up a huge bite of steaming salmon. "No offense, girly. I've had enough cans of soup to last me the rest of my life."

Just the thought of hearty beef and vegetable had her groaning, too. The sound quickly morphed into a sigh when she tasted the heavenly dish Logan had whipped up as if it were nothing. "Not going to complain there. You're hired, Logan-kun."

"Welcome home." Ben smiled then focused on devouring his dinner.

Kyana and Logan exchanged a smile over his head.

"Careful. I know the fire chief cleared this section of the structure. Still, I don't like the way the beams were compromised." Logan bounced on a spot that looked a little suspect. It creaked yet held.

"Then why don't you wait downstairs?" Kyana glanced over at his mammoth frame. "I'm not exactly a bean pole, but I'm a hell of a lot lighter than you."

"Hey." He paused his inspection to pat his six-pack abs. "This is all muscle, babe."

Kyana rolled her eyes. "No shit. You're so damn hard, you make a lousy pillow."

"I didn't hear any complaints last night or the night before or the night before that." His infectious grin made her wish she were close enough to smack him in the shoulder. Their friendship had picked up right where it had left off all those years ago.

Still, she didn't bother to argue. Neither one of them had scrambled very hard to find alternate sleeping arrangements. An afternoon or two could have emptied out the spare room in Rose's house to give them each a private spot. Both of them had clung to every available excuse to keep from going to the effort.

"Hell, last night you crashed before I even finished telling you about how me and Jerry Lu got the cow onto the roof of the school. You pestered me for months about that one back in the day. Ben says you're an insomniac. I think he's nuts. I mean, it's not every day a woman conks out in my bed. Well, your bed. Whatever. You know what I mean." He grinned. "Besides, you're not supposed to *sleep* on the hard parts. There are better uses for those."

She hoped he'd interpret her *harrumph* as feminist indignation rather than the self-annoyance that spawned the sound. Because although she knew his teasing was meant to be harmless fun, she couldn't help but wish he was serious.

"How about you put yourself to better use right now."

He strode toward her with no hesitation. "Here?"

"Where else?" She tried not to laugh when he neared. "Boost me up so I can grab those wicker baskets off the top shelf of the closet. I'm pretty sure that's where Ben meant he kept the fireproof box with the insurance paperwork. The sooner we get this red tape handled, the sooner we can start on repairs. It kills him not to be here, to know it's not all perfect and shiny. He loves this place."

"Yeah. Of course." Logan grimaced as he adjusted himself not so subtly.

Kyana should probably feel bad for triggering his instincts. She didn't. She enjoyed playing the siren, even if he would have had the same reaction to any available woman. Was waking up next to another warm body having the same effect on him as it was on her? The last time she'd been this horny she'd ended up hooking up with a friend of a friend at a backyard barbeque and making a pact with herself that other lawyers were off limits ever after. Each time she saw the scumbag in court, her bad judgment haunted her and his leer inspired the urge to shower.

Before she could brace herself against the hormonal surge Logan caused every time he touched her, he surrounded her waist with his broad fingers and lifted her several feet off the ground. She squeaked when he adjusted his grip, palming her ass with one hand and steadying her with the other.

"Don't worry. I'm not about to drop you. Ben would kick my ass." He laughed. "What's in there?"

Ignoring the heat of his contact, which seared through her jeans, she reached up and grabbed the tallest crate off the stack. When she tipped it forward, a grey metal box shifted. The heavy object threw off her balance and she wobbled.

"Whoa. Easy up there." Logan held true to his word. He compensated, but began to lower her.

"I think this is it. Put me down." She squirmed a bit, eager to verify the contents.

"Hmmm. I don't know." Logan gripped her tighter. "I kind of like the view from here."

"Oh my God. How old are you?" A half-hearted kick of her heel bounced off his steely ribs.

"Old enough to know what to do with a woman as gorgeous as you." He allowed her to sink a few more feet, inch by tantalizing inch. His hands were everywhere on her and she couldn't honestly say she hoped he'd hurry. "Pamper her, worship her, ravish her. Those are pretty high on my To Do list."

As soon as her sneakers hit the ground, he rotated her in his grip, relieving her of the basket, which he set to the side before crowding her against the closet wall. Instead of claustrophobia, a sense of protection settled over her.

"You're killing me, Ky." He surprised her by burying his nose in her hair and breathing deep. "This smell…"

"Stale smoke turns you on?" Being a smartass was pretty much her only defense at this point. This might be a game to him, but if she lost, she might never recover.

"Your shampoo, I've never forgotten how much I loved it." He grimaced. "I spent a while looking awkward once, sniffing a bunch of different kinds from the grocery store, but didn't find the right one by the time the manager walked past me for the third time so I gave up. They must have thought I was nuts."

"It's a salon brand. My mother used to buy it." She squinted up at him, trying to tell if he was serious. The dim light in the space made it impossible to tell what emotions clouded his deep blue eyes.

"Figures." He shook his head. "You always were too classy for me."

"What the hell is that supposed to mean?" She twined her fingers through the belt loops of his jeans when he would have retreated.

"You know damn well what I'm talking about." He looked away from her though there wasn't anything else to see in the tight confinement. "I'm a mutt, you're a purebred. You deserve a shit ton better than me."

"Logan!" She clawed him when fury flexed her fingers unwillingly. "You think I'm some kind of snob? What the hell did I ever do to give you that impression?"

"You?" He tilted his head, coming to peer at her again. "Nothing. It's just the facts. Even if you've never seemed to realize it. Why the hell do you think I left? It's water under the bridge, but you had to realize how close you came to tangoing with trash that last summer. Those last weeks. I wasn't about to let you make that kind of mistake with someone like me."

"Holy shit. You moron." She shook him, though he didn't budge an inch. "All this time... I thought you were awkward with me because I tricked you into kissing me. That you were too kind to say no. And then our friendship was shot to hell when I made you uncomfortable around me. Are you saying—?"

"You *what*?" He dipped down until only a tiny gap separated them.

Kyana couldn't help it. Her body went lax and allowed him to press closer.

"You seriously thought I didn't want you? That *you* took advantage of the situation?" He growled as he settled against her fully. "How could you have mistaken the way I looked at you like I wanted to devour you? I couldn't hide it at all anymore. I left before I did something selfish and trapped you here with me. You were going places. Big places. And I sure as shit wasn't about to be the reason you threw all that potential away. It wasn't right. We were like family, Ben said it himself. But there I was, thinking really impure thoughts. And you were so young."

"We're the same damn age, asshole." She slapped her palms on his chest. He didn't flinch. Instead he leaned inward, trapping her hands between them.

"Maybe technically. But I'd had a shit ton more experience than you back then. You had no idea what the real world was like." He shook his head. "How judgmental and cruel it can be. How unfair."

"Seriously?" She would have slapped him if she could have moved. "My fucking parents were killed, stolen from me before I could even really understand how amazing they were."

"They didn't *choose* to abandon you, Ky." He swallowed hard. "Not like my mom."

"You know how I feel about that. She didn't deserve you anyway. That's beside the point. Don't you think being orphaned was a rude awakening for me, too? Sure, I had Aunt Rose. I loved her. I'm not saying I didn't. But... Really, you don't remember all the times you held me when I cried for them? Did you think that was some kind of act?"

"Shit. Sorry." He tilted his head forward until his forehead rested on hers. "That's not what I meant. Not exactly. See this is part of the problem. I can never make you understand without setting you off or jacking things up. I only wanted to protect you. Even if that meant from myself."

"You moron." The heat had vanished from her insults. "Don't you realize how bad you hurt me by walking away? Who was there to save me from the pain of losing my best friend? The guy I had my first crush on? No one. I never felt so forsaken in my life. Not even after the accident. I missed you. Every day. And since Rose… Well, it's been horrible again. I hate being alone. I don't want to be on my own anymore. You're the only guy who's ever really understood me. Don't do that to me again."

"What?" He flinched as if she'd kneed him in the nuts.

"I wanted you Logan. You pushed me away. When you didn't stick around…it almost killed me. And Ben. I was embarrassed and guilty as hell for stealing you from him. If I'd just kept from stirring things up, you wouldn't have had to go."

"Fuck," he snarled. "See what I mean? I have the un-Midas touch. Everything I do turns to shit. You make me sound like my freaking mom, cutting and running. What the hell should I have done?"

"Why not keep it simple? Maybe more of this would have helped." She smiled the instant before her lips met his. Unlike the timid girl she'd been, she didn't give him a chance to evade and escape. She balled her fists in his T-shirt and kept him close while she took what she craved and gave all she had pent up.

Logan didn't resist. He hummed, deep in his throat, when she flicked her tongue over the seam of his lips. Then he parted them, letting her have the lead. His control lasted longer than she'd guessed it might. For a solid thirty seconds, he allowed her to play—explore, taste and plunder as she saw fit. His gaze never left hers, though his hands began to wander up her hips, careful to skim her injuries as if he'd memorized every bump and bruise the night he'd had her laid out naked before him.

When she nipped his bottom lip, he broke.

Pinned between the wall and his chest, she had no way to evade the sensual assault he captained. Why the hell would she want to?

She reveled in the advancement of his torso, which imposed on the entire surface of her front. Warmth radiated from him, making her curl into the welcome heat of his embrace. He separated them just enough to allow her to wind her arms around his neck when she wiggled then fused them even more completely, if such a thing were possible.

He fit her just right.

Tall, she'd sometimes had trouble finding a guy who could manage to make her feel dainty and feminine. Logan had no problem there. He towered over her and consumed her with his presence. She clung to him, her thigh rubbing the outside of his hip as she practically climbed the trunk of his body. Anything to get at the honey and ginger taste of his lips, sweetened by the loose-leaf tea he'd sipped from one of Rose's china cups earlier.

The memory of his huge hands cradling the delicate vessel ratcheted her desire higher. Just like he did for her when he grasped her leg at her knee. His fingers teased the underside, and trapped her against his hip. She hopped, wrapping her other leg high around his waist.

Both of them moaned when he fit himself to the juncture of her thighs, settling into the soft cradle she made for him. There they were entirely opposite, his cock so hard against her mound she wondered if it ached. Writhing against him served several purposes. Like rubbing the diamond tips of her breasts on his firm chest and soothing some of the restlessness pervading her. Mostly though, the action helped her snuggle as tight as possible to him, right where she had dreamt of being for so long that no other guy had lived up to her high expectations, established in one decade-old itty bitty kiss.

He sucked her tongue into his mouth, capturing the sensitive muscle then stroking it with his own. When he retreated, she nearly cried out. But only for a moment. Until he laid open-mouthed kisses at the corner of her lips, across her chin then in a meandering path along the exposed length of her neck as her head dropped back.

With a *thunk* it hit the wall of the closet, startling them both.

"Let's take this somewhere a little more comfy? Somewhere we can stretch out." He didn't wait for her answer. Covering her mouth again in a drugging kiss, he kept her from warning him as he hauled her backwards. The basket she'd set on the floor loomed behind him. She struggled, but he misinterpreted the message. He chuckled. "I know, Ky. Me too. Just a second. Promise."

His unexpected sweetness made it twice as hard to bear when he tripped over their bounty. He cursed. With the reflexes of a cat, he twisted, taking the brunt of the impact on his shoulders. Though it had to hurt like hell, he didn't flinch, making sure to shelter her from any residual force. Their heads knocked together. Other than that and their pride, they appeared unscathed.

"Jesus." Logan banded his arms around her and rolled. From her new angle, beneath him, she spied the basket teetering precariously. Sure enough, it toppled. With a crash, the fireproof box tumbled to the floor and papers spilled out everywhere.

"What the fuck just happened here?" The dazed confusion in his bedroom eyes had her feeling a tad bit smug.

"I think we almost made it to second base but got tagged out." She winked.

A strangled laugh fell from his sexy smile. "Right. I got that part. Damn lockbox."

"Very secure too." Kyana wriggled from beneath Logan's heavy, though not uncomfortable, frame. She inspected the case, which had divulged all its contents. "I suppose that's what happens when you leave the key in the damn lock."

"Figures." Logan shook his head. "I'm surprised Ben didn't have the papers stuffed in a shoebox under the bed. That's what I would have done."

"Actually, I'm pretty sure he did." She dredged up a hazy memory. "But Aunt Rose bought him the fireproof box for Christmas one year, then guilted him into using it so it wouldn't go to waste."

"Brilliant. Man, I miss her." He reached for Kyana's hand, interlacing their fingers. "I'm so sorry. I should have been here. For both of you."

"I understand, Logan-kun." She raised his knuckles to her lips and dusted a kiss over them. "Rose did too. She told me to tell you she loves you. And that she's proud of the man you turned out to be."

"She did?" His whole body tensed and his eyes glistened.

"Of course." Kyana tugged him to her and nestled into his open arms. "You were like the son she never had. She bragged about you to anyone who would listen."

"Damn. That's...nice." He cleared his throat.

She granted him a bit of privacy, angling away so she could shuffle through the documents littering the closet floor. The insurance policy was easy to spot. Thick folded papers from Salem Mutual had dog-eared corners and a distinctly yellow cast. After plucking them from the wreckage, the rest of the stationary caught her attention.

Finely written cursive swirled over botanical prints. Dozens of letters had been protected from the blaze along with the deed to Ben's house and the title to his car.

"What are those?" Logan peeked over her shoulder as she ran one fingertip across the fine linens.

"Looks like Rose's handwriting. They must have been pen pals for a while. Maybe when Ben took the third shift as a security guard at the oven factory. He always claimed to be bored silly. I remember my great aunt saying she hated him being gone so much. They really were close friends." Kyana sighed. "I think she once even offered to pay off Ben's house so he wouldn't have to work so hard."

"Like he'd have gone for that!" Logan looked horrified.

"Some things are more important than money, don't you think?" She tilted her head. "Like relationships? You can't buy them."

"Are you saying...? I mean, do you think Rose and Ben...?" He waved his hands adorably in the space between them as his eyes grew wide.

"Actually, no. I don't." She shook her head slowly. "But I *have* often wondered if they might have been more to each other if given the chance."

The instant denial she'd sort of expected didn't materialize. Logan weighed her opinion before shooting it down. He always did. "You know, I think you might be right. Ben never brought women around, though I know he took lovers from time to time. They would call sometimes. He never really dated them though. Never invited them here. I always thought that was odd, but not if he cared for Rose. It sort of makes sense if he didn't want to rub her face in it."

Kyana concentrated on rewrapping the bundle of letters with the pretty lilac ribbon that'd fallen off them. She didn't look up when she said, "It would have killed her to see him with someone else."

"Not something she should have worried about." Logan wrapped his hand around hers on the package. "Ben would never have hurt her like that."

And somehow Kyana knew his great-nephew wouldn't be so crass either. Thank God. She'd claw out the eyes of any woman he brought to their home.

"Ky, before you finish that bow, I think there's another piece of paper under the lid." He deflected them from the awkward stream of conversation.

She reached in the direction he indicated. Instantly, she felt the difference. This rough stock had nothing in common with Rose's refined parchment. Squinting, she examined the typed document.

If she hadn't been a lawyer, the thing might as well have been penned in Martian. As it was, the age of the contract made the verbiage difficult to discern. Not to mention property law wasn't her specialty. Good thing she had a friend in the business. She was going to need some help.

"What's that frown for?" Logan encroached on her space.

She didn't mind. "Sorry. This is some kind of title addendum stipulating conditional sale clauses."

"Come again?" He scratched his head.

"Unless I was really distracted, we haven't gotten there yet."

"Ha ha. No, seriously. Tell me what it means? In English. Simple terms for a simple guy."

"Quit that. You're plenty smart. It says Ben took a discount on the sale of the house that gave the builder options to buy back certain easement rights. For up to fifty years. I'm not sure I get all the nuances, but something like if the house wasn't standing, they could reclaim the land." A knot of unease lodged in her guts.

"What's the date on that thing?" Logan seemed to jump to the same conclusions.

"Fifty and a half years ago. Give or take a month."

"Wouldn't that mean it was null and void?" He looked to her.

"Probably. Yeah." She shrugged. "But who knows how accurate someone might be if they thought they knew what was in here. It'd be easy to flub something by a few months after all this time, right?"

The both scrambled to their feet.

Logan clutched her wrist even as he looked over their shoulders. Where Kyana had felt entirely secure a moment ago, hairs on her neck rose and goose bumps pimpled her flesh. "We're getting the hell out of here. Hand me the box and stay behind me. Close."

There was no use arguing when he made up his mind. "I know somebody who can help. I'll scan this and email it over to him right away."

"Sounds like a plan." They were breathing hard for an entirely different reason when they emerged into the grey haze of dusk.

Kyana was glad for Logan's strong grip on her hand when she caught movement out of the corner of her eye and skidded to a stop. He halted with her, spinning until he faced the offender that inspired her pulse to speed like a racecar driver heading for the checkered flag.

Daryl Thick.

"Jesus," Logan muttered under his breath as his hackles fell into place and the instant alertness of his body relaxed.

The ex-military man ran a hand through his buzz cut and flashed them a quick salute before jogging toward his house with a few glances thrown over his ripped shoulders. It might be easy to dismiss his presence as a man out for an evening stroll, if he hadn't popped up from behind Ben's hedge like Rambo's pet gopher.

"What do you think he was doing in there?" she whispered to Logan.

"No fucking clue." He shrugged. "We can discuss it inside. Where it's safe. Let's go."

She leaned against his side when he wrapped his free arm around her shoulders and tugged her impossibly near. "Won't hear me arguing. Besides, I want to know what Ben has to say about this stupid contract."

"You and me both, Kyana-chan."

CHAPTER FOUR

Kyana, both relieved and oddly disappointed, stared at the email glowing on her screen. It had taken almost a week for her friend to completely vet the option clause on Ben's house. The good news... Logan had gotten it correct. No matter what crazy agreement the man had signed to afford his dream home, it was irrelevant today. The expiration date had passed without the rights being exercised. The house and the land belonged to Logan's great uncle free and clear.

So why had the fire investigator's report shown hints of arson? Ben swore he never used candles, yet there had been one set unwisely close to the curtains Rose had sewn as a birthday gift for him back in the seventies. The hideous polyester had gone up like a match, destroying one of Ben's prized possessions along with kindling the blaze. He insisted he only kept the pillars on hand for emergencies. So who had known where he stashed them, retrieved one and lit the damn thing? And why?

In addition to all that, Kyana wished she could hash things out with Logan. He'd spent every waking minute working on the house since the release had come through the morning after their close call in the closet. Hell, she'd hardly seen him in days. No wonder her insomnia had returned full force. Without him to cuddle up to, the darkness summoned all sorts of demons to torture her awake. And when he finally stumbled in—exhausted—each night, he barely managed to undress and shower before falling into a near coma.

She'd offered to play his assistant. He'd refused, probably since she'd upheld her end of the stupid bargain by fronting cash and drafting a work agreement. Or maybe because he regretted their momentary lapse of decorum between Ben's flannel shirts.

All she knew for sure was that from her window she had a world-class view of him going to town on his great uncle's kitchen—sans shirt of course. An unseasonable heatwave had crept up on the heels of their mild winter, spiking the temperature into the lower nineties several days in a row. The hot spell coincided with the demolition phase of the project, providing ample opportunity to showcase Logan's sweaty muscles, which glistened as they flexed beneath the strain of his efforts.

Fancy molding around the window dug into Kyana's hip as she leaned against the casing. With the lights off, she'd moved aside the lace curtains for a clear view of her obsession. How healthy could this be? Next she'd be sharing the hedge with Daryl for a better perspective.

Hopefully Logan would smile instead of cringing when she took them down memory lane. At this point she'd rather know where they stood than hanging around wondering any longer. Making a clean break would be tough the more time she spent near him. This was what she wanted, and she wasn't about to wait for him this go around.

Hoping her initiative went over as well tonight as it had the other day, she grasped the metal cylinder tighter between her shaking fingers. With her thumb, she slid the switch. A dull red glow emanated from the end of the flashlight, mostly covered by her hand.

She grinned despite the stuttering of her heartbeat as she remembered all the nights they'd sent messages across the canyon between their great aunt and uncle's houses. Kids who texted on cell phones or messaged on iStuff or posted on Facebook wouldn't know what they were missing.

Sure, she could have called Logan, but what fun would that be?

Chuckling, she aimed the flashlight toward Ben's house then removed and replaced her hand.

Short. Long. Short. Short.

Dot. Dash. Dot. Dot.

Morse code for "L".

The signal had always made her think of Gotham City paging Batman. In a lot of ways, Logan had been her superhero. Maybe still was.

He'd swooped in and improved her life both back then and again recently. When she'd needed him most, he had her back.

It'd probably take a while to draw his attention from the task at hand—ripping out the toasted bones of the cabinetry. Or at least, she'd thought it would. A gasp escaped when he spun to face her window immediately. She repeated the signal. From that distance she could barely make out his broad smile when he realized what had caused the glint.

He held up his palm, then lunged for his battered toolbox, presenting her with a view of his gorgeous, jeans-clad ass. In less than five seconds, he'd returned.

Dash dash. Dot dot. Dot dot dot. Dot dot dot. Pause. Dash dash. Dot.

"*Miss me?*"

Arrogant prick. And right on the money. Damn him.

Dash dot. Dash dash dash.

"*No.*"

She could have sworn she spied him laughing when he sent his next message.

Dot dash dot dot. Dot dot. Dot dash. Dot dash dot.

"*Liar.*"

No use in denying it.

Dash dot dash dash. Dot. Dot dot dot.

"*Yes.*"

She'd barely finished the last letter when he sent her the invitation she'd been hoping for.

Dash dot dash dot. Dash dash dash. Dash dash. Dot. Pause. Dot dot dot dot. Dot. Dot dash dot. Dot.

"Come here."

Kyana flashed one last note, both agreement and her closing initial, before wrapping her gossamer robe around her and sprinting for the door.

Dash dot dash.

"K."

She shouldn't have been surprised when the beam of his light intersected hers from his spot on Ben's deck. Even back in high school, he hadn't allowed her to make the miniscule voyage solo. Heaven forbid she twist her ankle or cross paths with a startled squirrel. Tonight she appreciated his supervision.

As she neared, she scrambled for something to say. Maybe she should have thought beyond the thrill of sharing some time and space with him. "So… How's it going?"

"You tell me. I'm sure you could monitor my progress from your perch by the window." He winked. "How long were you going to lurk there and peep?"

"How did you spot me?" Mortified, she pressed her fingers to her flaming cheeks.

"I didn't. But I could feel your stare on me." He buffed his arms. "You're distracting me, Ky. I nearly smashed my thumb with that last cabinet."

"Sorry." She stammered.

"I liked it." He tugged her into his grasp. Even perspiring, he smelled clean and manly. She had to stop herself from sinking her teeth into the tight pec in front of her lips. "I need a break anyway. It's hot as hell in there. If I add you to that sauna, the windows will steam up for sure."

"Yeah, right." She glanced away.

"I'm serious, Ky." He nudged her chin up with his thumb and index finger. "You're the sexiest woman I've ever met. At least now I don't have to feel like a perv for thinking so."

"What the hell are you talking about?" She tilted her head, dragging his fingers across her chin.

"When I visited, I liked to think of Ben and Rose and you as my family." He shrugged then rubbed at the spot he'd touched as though wiping away some imaginary stain. "When I started to have other feelings, I freaked. The first time I had a dirty dream about you, I couldn't talk to you for two days. It seemed wrong to go from thinking of you as a little sister—hanging out with you, keeping you out of trouble and giving you noogies to... Well, you know."

"Not really." She took his hand in hers and started to amble down the private walkway in the direction of the woods behind their houses, tugging him along with her. "I mean, *if* there had been something more between us, don't you think most of our foundation would have stayed the same? We'd still be friends first, right?"

"I guess. But that's a more mature rationale than I was capable of then. I couldn't stop thinking about how I'd kick my ass if I were anyone else trying to put moves on you. Though hell, I never was much good at the keeping-you-trouble-free part. You're just too damn good at finding shit to get into."

"Ha. I don't find it. *It* finds *me* all on its own. Remember that blue T-shirt with the sparkly iron-on Ben bought me after we crashed our toboggan into his shed during winter break? It said so." She liked that their steps synchronized without effort.

"Right." He shook his head and laughed. "You loved that damn thing. But yeah, even all this time later I still want to hang out with you, see movies, grill on nice nights, play board games when it rains, and bake you a birthday cake every year. All the crap we did when we were younger. Those were the happiest times of my life, Ky. Maybe this go around I could even spring for a nice dinner when it's in my budget."

His frown spurred her to go for broke. If they didn't iron out some of their wrinkles, they wouldn't have a chance at making it long term. A fling with him didn't interest her. It would only screw up everything else they shared. A friendship she wasn't willing to risk. Not when she'd just found it again.

"Why don't you let *me* take *you* out sometime?" She gnawed on the inside of her cheek, hoping he'd trust her and grow just a little.

"I don't know..." He looked like he was grinding his teeth for a minute before he sighed.

"Money is worthless if I can't enjoy it. Spending time with you, eating fine cuisine and maybe sharing a nice bottle of wine sounds like a perfect evening. Would you keep us both from experiencing it just to bolster your pride? Who picks up the tab doesn't mean anything, Logan. Not if we're talking about you and me trying to be an *us*. Is that what we're discussing?"

"Damn, you really did grow a pair. A bigger pair, I guess. You always were bold." He wiggled his eyebrows. "I like this new Kyana. You're turning me on."

"You didn't answer my question." She would have tapped her toe if they had been standing still. If he left her hanging now, all her sudden confidence would melt away.

"Only because you're diverting the blood flow from my brain." He scowled before taking a funny stride to give his junk more room in the confines of his ripped jeans. "Yes. I'm doing my best to charm you into dating me. Is it working?"

"Not like you have to try very hard. Probably never have had to do more than crook your finger to get a woman. But if we're going to have a real shot, we have to fix the things we did wrong last time. We can't rewind but we can redo. I'm trying to be brave here. So don't say no."

"I hate it when you make sense," he grumbled.

"I'm not a kickass lawyer for nothing. Logic is my business, buddy." She poked him in the side. "So it's a date?"

"Hell yeah." He turned to her with a grin. "Things on my new and improved list to try... Number one, let my sugar mama take me out for a juicy porterhouse and get sloshed on fancy-pants booze. Now, about those noogies. Hmm... haven't done that to a girl in a while."

She yelped and dodged his swipe, shaking her hand free of his.

He humored her by letting her trot ahead down the illuminated path. The solar lights Ben had installed on either side of the river rock would glow softly for hours yet. When her breath came in short pants and her robe fluttered behind her, she slowed. Right on her heels, Logan grabbed her around the waist and tugged her backward into his chest.

"I remember this. Playing. Laughing. Effortless enjoyment. Carefree joy when we were together," he whispered in her ear, not the least bit winded. "I've missed this. You."

Kyana angled her head enough to grant him permission for more. He accepted the offer.

Cupping her cheek in his palm, he guided her to his mouth. Gently, they exchanged a soft kiss before separating with a sigh. It was as if he had the same idea she did. The same destination in mind. If there was anything she wanted a repeat performance of—a chance to rewrite—it was the night they'd done *almost* this. They started down the path together again, allowing a buffer between them to keep them from ripping each other's clothes off where they stood.

After a few seconds, Logan cleared his throat.

"Remember how we used to help Myrtle gather her leaves every fall? We'd pile them so high we could jump off her porch railing into the mess before she'd chase us off and scoop them into the burning barrel." He sighed. "At least you always took the plunge. I was jealous as I got older and watched from the sidelines."

"I wouldn't have judged you for acting like a kid." She hugged him with one arm as they rounded a bend beneath the canopy woven from the green shoots of old trees, which reminded her of the new season of her relationship with Logan. It had been a hard winter for them both.

Fall seemed like a long way off, but soon enough the same plants would be red and gold and crispy. Perfect for frolicking in. A mental note would remind her to force Logan to join her this time.

"I know, you never looked down on me like a lot of the other kids in school when I didn't show up wearing anything that had been fashionable in this century and my lunch got paid for by the state. I guess I just learned to fend for myself with my mom never around and it got harder to let go of the tough-guy act. I was afraid I wouldn't be able to give up the luxury when I had to survive on my own again." He groaned. "I sound like some nutcase on Dr. Phil."

"You don't watch that shit, do you?" She cracked up.

"Hell no, but you get the point."

"I do." She nibbled at the corner of her mouth as a structure coalesced from the shadows. The dock at the edge of the pond. Thank goodness the moon was bright. Or maybe if it had been dimmer she'd have more nerve.

"Are we really going to do this?" He rubbed the sensitive skin between her thumb and forefinger. "Are you sure you're ready?"

"I never was the kind of person to dip a toe in. If we're going to do this, let's make a splash. Okay?" She squeezed her eyes closed as she waited what seemed like an eternity for his response.

"Shit, yes." He sped up, dragging her along. "Only this time, I want to do more than swim with you, Ky. A hell of a lot more."

"Thank God." She kicked off her sneakers mid-stride as they reached the first weathered planks.

"One thing though…" He stopped mid-stride. "I, uh, don't make a habit of carrying condoms on me. I didn't expect you to step out of my fantasy tonight."

"Oh." She blinked. "Damn. I'm not on the pill or anything. It's sort of been a while for me."

"I'm not going to lie." He smiled. "I like the sound of that. Don't worry, Ky. I can still take care of you. I always will."

Tripping seemed like a very real possibility when Logan flicked open the button on his jeans and spread the fly wide. A trail of fine, dark hair drew her gaze downward.

"If your eyes get any bigger, babe…"

"Bigger? Not in this lifetime." A well-placed smack on his tight abs echoed through the stillness.

Logan grabbed her wrist and used it to draw her near. "Now, that wasn't very nice."

She fought half-heartedly against his grip. "What are you going to do about it?"

"Maybe I'll spank you later." He growled. "But for now I think this will do."

A squeak escaped her parted lips when he shoved the robe from her shoulders then grasped the hem of her silk tank and whipped it over her head in one lightning-fast move. Her matching boyshorts didn't last much longer. And before she could panic, he'd stripped her naked.

"Damn, you're beautiful." He sank to his knees at her feet.

Kyana shifted, awkward in the beam of his attention. It shone brighter than her flashlight had earlier, exposing all her flaws.

"Why don't you believe me?" He grasped her hips, his thumbs stroking maddeningly over the curves of the bones there while he kissed the soft swell of the belly she couldn't erase no matter how often she worked out. Probably because she had a weakness for cupcake-flavored ice cream. How could she resist the veins of icing and sprinkles swirled inside it?

She'd loved it since she'd been a child.

Some things never changed. Like her feelings for the man in front of her, whom she was pretty sure she adored even more than ice cream.

"It's not that I don't feel good about myself." She buried her fingers in his hair to keep upright when his wandering caresses invoked dizziness. "It's just that you're...perfect. You should be dating a supermodel or something."

He laughed so hard the pattern of his touches stuttered.

She smacked his shoulder. "I mean it."

"You have a way of making me feel like so much more than I am." He grew still as he peered up at her from his place at her feet. "I love the way you do that. Pump me up. Always have. Thank you."

"I only treat you like you deserve." She rubbed her thumb over his damp lips.

"Let me do the same for you, Ky." He sucked the digit into his mouth, thrilling her with the heat and pressure of his gentle sucking. "I'll give you everything I can. I swear."

"Then how about losing those jeans." She gulped. "Let me see you again."

"I'll let you do a hell of a lot more than that." He rose and shucked the denim before she could brace herself for the impact of his bare-naked glory.

When his cock fell free, thick and heavy against his thigh, she nearly drooled. The unseasonably balmy night had nothing on the way he made her overheat. If she didn't do something to cool off she'd explode. "First you'll have to catch me."

She sprinted for the edge of the platform and dove into the water, relying on muscle memory from the million times she'd executed the maneuver in their past to guide her. Cool, refreshing water sluiced over her body—face, hands and bare breasts. When her lungs began to burn, she surfaced, throwing her head back to clear the wet hair from her eyes.

"Christ, you look like a mermaid." Logan muttered from the dock.

She was a little disappointed he hadn't joined her until he perched on the edge of the structure. Wicked ideas swam into her mind. She tipped onto her back, stroking until she floated by his shins. His skin was tan even in the moonlight.

"Now that's a sight I'll never forget." He muttered oaths and curses into the night.

"Testing the water, Logan?" She teased him for his slower method of entry.

"I'm not sure shocking the boys is the right approach when I'm trying to make a good first impression." He grimaced at the thought of the cool liquid.

She grinned, letting her legs sink until she treaded water between his knees. Then she walked her dripping fingers up his legs, using him to anchor her. He'd always done that for her. When she reached his thighs, he shivered.

"Whatcha doing, Ky?"

"Playing." She peered up at him as she buoyed at the surface, her lips now following the path her fingers had taken. "You won't spoil my fun, will you?"

"Too much of that and you'll ruin it yourself." He groaned.

"You can handle it." She nipped the sinew of his inner thigh. His hands fisted at his side a moment before reaching under her arms to help her stay afloat while she explored. He tasted amazing. Like early summer and salt and man. "Besides, if there are no condoms in your wallet, you might as well let me solve this problem another way or you're likely to hurt yourself walking home."

"Never had my hard-on referred to as a problem before." He scowled adorably.

"Really? Fitting all that inside seems like it would be a delicate operation." She measured him with a slow circuit using the tip of her finger. "I've certainly never been with a guy your size before."

"We'll go slow when the time comes. It'll work just fine, I promise." He lost his breath as she considered the possibilities.

After reaching up to band her arms around his waist and lay her head in his lap, she hesitated. Near her prize, her breath washed over the incredibly long, thick shaft of his cock. From here she could spot a bead of wetness at the tip. She licked her lips.

"You're killing—" His declaration ended in a gurgle when she lapped at the head of his erection with the flat of her tongue, savoring the flavor of him. Slowly and sweetly, she dusted him with kisses before drawing him into her mouth. When she'd taken as much as she could without choking, she began to suck in a series of soft, delicate swallows. The thrill of new and different sensations magnified her natural excitement. This was Logan. And it was really happening.

Not intending to race to the finish, she reveled in his surrender and set herself to granting him as much pleasure as she could. Because if she knew him at all, he wouldn't take for himself very long before returning the favor. A million times over.

Cicadas helped her keep a rhythm, her head bobbing delicately over her treat. It amazed her to finally have him in her grasp. And to be thrilling him. Because the noises bubbling from his sexy chest were clear indications he was enjoying himself.

Immensely.

Her hands wandered up and down his furred thighs as she grew more comfortable with his girth, which spread her jaw wide. She kicked her feet lazily to assist her in the natural bobbing motion she required. The cool water and the warm night combined to awaken every nerve ending in her skin.

At the first flick of her tongue over the sensitive underside of his tip, Logan hauled her upward as though she weighed no more than a legal-sized notepad. He held her suspended, half-submerged, far enough away from him that she had to stop her teasing.

"Maybe I had my strategy all wrong." Husky whispers thrilled her. Could she really have done that to his voice? "I should have realized that with you, I'm going to need all the help I can get to restrain myself from ending this party before it starts."

"Don't hold back." She wriggled until her belly brushed his erection, encouraging his surrender. "I want to make you crazy."

"You can check that box. Fucking great." He scooted closer to the edge and lowered her until she could feed more of his shaft between her lips when she descended again. Still she couldn't take the whole thing. Instead she wrapped her hand around the base of his cock and massaged in time with the ministrations of her mouth. "This is going to be embarrassingly easy for you."

"Mmm." She hummed against his shaft, loving the flex that followed the vibrations.

"Damn. Yes." He twined his fingers in her hair, guiding her in the rhythm he preferred. "Just like that, Ky. Better than I imagined."

Tracing each vein with her tongue, she studied his topography. Therefore, she caught the difference right away when he grew impossibly harder and the ridges became more pronounced.

"I'm going to..."

She added a twist of her head as she rose off his throbbing cock before plunging down once more. Faster and harder, she suckled him as jets of come blasted from his plum-shaped tip. Water splashed as his legs kicked, his feet breaking the surface when his hips began an involuntary thrusting. His whole body moved sinuously, making her sure she wanted to experience his release from beneath that amazing frame someday. Soon.

His muscles flexed, then trembled. He slumped, breathing as hard as if he'd just carried ten loads of supplies from his truck to a job site on the fifth floor of an apartment building with no elevator.

Petting his flank, she rested against him, smiling while he recovered.

"You look awfully proud of yourself." If she were a cat, she would have purred when he petted her hair then traced her lips, swiping the last bit of fluid from them.

"Shouldn't I be?" She peeked up at him from behind her lashes.

"Hell yeah." He reached for her, drawing her out of the water completely this time.

Droplets rained from her skin, dripping onto him. He seemed to relish the relief from the heat, and tugged her closer until he nearly singed her with his torso. His arms wrapped around her, holding her tight to him as he leaned in to claim her mouth.

Kyana had never been kissed like this— tender yet rough, gentle yet insistent, carnal yet sweet. She could have kept going forever. All the while, his hands roamed her back from shoulders to ass, spiraling her need higher until a whimper escaped her.

"You're pretty when you beg, Ky," he murmured against her neck before nipping her there just hard enough to have her arching in his hold. Her breasts rubbed against his chest, stimulating her diamond-hard nipples.

"I did no such thing." She tried to deny it. No use.

"Your body is speaking for you." He smiled, long and slow. "Don't worry, I'm listening."

She sighed when he separated them enough to turn, setting her on the dock with one last deep kiss. Then he entered the pond without a splash. The power and grace of his well-muscled shoulders and ass left her in awe. With him beneath the silvery surface, which glinted in the moonlight, she thought maybe she'd imagined the entire interlude.

Until he rose from the depths like a mythical creature designed to lure her into temptation. A male siren. She'd willingly fall into his trap. Any price would be worth the paradise he promised with a sweltering stare and the curve of his sexy smile as he swam back.

"Come closer." He tugged on her ankle until she perched with her ass on the edge of the dock. "Lay back."

She did as he instructed without argument. He might as well have charmed her like a snake in a basket for all she wished to disobey.

"That's right. Stay on your elbows so you can watch me. I want you to see how much I enjoy pleasuring you." He lifted one of her feet from the silky water.

Logan tagged a kiss to her arch before beginning a slow press and release of his fingers that quickly turned into a full-on massage. Her toes curled when he rubbed her just right. Having mastered that part of her anatomy, he proceeded to climb to her ankles.

"Will you wear heels for me when we go on our date?" He licked the skin there. "I'm picturing you in a power suit and killer stilettos. Your hair back, no nonsense. I can't explain how hot your lawyer pictures made me when I spotted them in Rose's house. Tell me you have some shoes tucked away with all that naughty lingerie you hoard."

"I might have a pair." She scooted at least three inches closer when he nibbled on her calf.

"Or twenty, I bet." He hummed against the inside of her knee, driving her mad.

"Who's counting?" The question barely snuck past the constriction of her throat and a similar squeeze on her heart. Could he really be here, delighting her?

To reassure herself, she petted his silky hair. So soft, even wet.

"Yeah, I'm not going anywhere." He read her mind. Then he blew it with a few well-placed swirls of his thumb over the apex of her slit. Not once did she consider closing her legs despite his intimate position, which would have unnerved her with any other man. Good thing awkwardness never entered the picture since he'd blocked the possibility of hiding by inserting his torso fully between her thighs. "I'm dying to taste you, Ky."

"Do it." She let her hands slide palms down on the wood behind her. On straight-locked arms, she leaned back. "Please."

Droplets ran down his chest when he hoisted himself up a few inches higher, enough to seal his mouth over the lips of her pussy, which shimmered in the moonlight, more from his influence than the refreshing liquid of the pond.

Kyana gasped.

His tongue insinuated itself between her lips and teased her swollen clit. A flutter, to preview his skill before he warmed her up with long laps and kisses on the ridges and valleys of her folds. Sure, guys had gone down on her before. None of them had performed with as much gusto as Logan. Never had a man made her feel like he enjoyed the act as much as she did.

Logan devoured her like the starving kid he'd been.

Not some sort of repayment for her blowjob, though she had to admit she'd done her best for him. Hell, he seemed satisfied to drive her wild if his hums of appreciation and approval were any indication.

The drumming of her heels on his shoulders forced him tighter to her core. He took the opportunity to prod her opening with the tip of one finger, pressing inward until he breached the tight rings of muscle at her entrance.

"Oh, fuck me." She blushed when she realized she'd shouted into the night.

"Next time, sweetheart." He nuzzled her softness, burrowing deeper with a simultaneous oral and manual assault. "I promise. I'll be the first guy in line at the pharmacy tomorrow."

Her giggle turned into a moan when he added a second finger then scissored them while he started that flicky thing with his tongue again. After that she couldn't think about anything other than the bliss he instilled in her and the magic of the moment. Holy shit, why hadn't they done this right the first time? They'd wasted a decade apart.

"Where'd you go, Ky?" Logan whispered against her mound before returning his attention to her—twice as fast, twice as intense.

"We lost so much time." She felt herself unraveling as he lifted her higher. Euphoria laced with regret made the triumph that much sweeter.

"We'll make up for it." He didn't pause longer than it took to utter the pledge.

Shudders began deep inside her, an early warning sign of the explosion brewing. When he looked up at her to gauge her reaction—or maybe to command her surrender—she got lost in his gorgeous blue eyes. The connection, so strong, pushed her over the edge.

She called out his name as wave after wave of ecstasy flooded her heart and soul along with her corporeal form. Endless pulses of pleasure transmitted waves through her muscles until she'd wrung every last drop of delight from the experience.

And when she had mostly stopped seizing, she realized he'd withdrawn gently from her body and levered himself onto their stage. He collapsed on his back and drew her to his side, where she curled up as if she'd done it a million times before. Sleeping with him the past week or so had ranked high on her list of lifetime achievements. Now his protective hold and his familiar warmth seemed even more welcoming.

"Feel better?" His husky voice proclaimed he knew he'd satisfied her.

"A little bit." She laughed when he tickled her. "Okay, yeah. A ton."

"Me too, Ky. Open your eyes. Check out all the fireflies." He drew her attention, encouraging her to blink open extra-heavy lids.

The view was worth it. Dozens of tiny stars winged around them, flickering on and off in a mating call she could certainly relate to. Hell, she half-expected to see her skin glowing when she glanced down.

Navy blue sky peeked through the shadow of the trees and warm yellow sparks dotted the landscape, highlighting the natural beauty all around them.

"I could stay like this forever." She hugged him, welcoming his echoing squeeze.

"I wish we could. Sorry, Ky. You're shivering." He kissed her forehead then sat up, hauling her with him. "Time for bed."

As if on cue, she yawned.

"Here, lift up." He slid her camisole over her arms then helped her step into her silk shorts and bundled her into the thin robe before collecting his pants. He shimmied into them with an adorable wiggle of his damp ass.

The contorted face he made when he spun around had her laughing out loud.

"Ugh. Everything's stuck together. Let's get home before this causes permanent damage." He stalked to her side. "Maybe we should take a shower together…"

She grabbed his hand and tugged as she slipped on her no-lace sneakers. "I'm pretty sure that's a good idea."

"Not sold?" He pinched her ass. "I must not have done this right, then."

"Oh, you did just fine." She winked. "But I think I need to try it again to be certain I like it."

"You're on." He lunged for her, swinging her into his arms as he took off, loping down the path back to the house.

When he jerked to a stop about halfway there, she squeaked.

"Shh." All his easy joy drained from his body, replaced by tension. "I thought I saw something."

"There are a bunch of deer that roam around this part of the property." She couldn't think of any other explanation. "Or maybe it's bigfoot."

"Not funny." He never once took his eyes from the general area he'd been scouting. He set her down and stepped in between her and the direction he'd peered. This time he raised his voice. "Who's out there?"

Kyana gripped his hand hard enough she feared she might break a bone or two. A heartbeat passed and then another before a cracking twig had them both jumping.

"It's just me, Logan." Daryl Thick stepped from the shadows. "You've got a good eye. I always told you to try the military."

"I still say I wasn't made to take orders. But I would like to know what the hell you're doing sneaking around all the time." His shoulders spread and his chest puffed up as he confronted the retired veteran.

Kyana was about to jump to the man's defense when he shocked the hell out of her.

"I was watching you two lovebirds."

Fists immediately formed at Logan's sides. "You did what?"

"Jesus, man." Daryl waved his hands in front of his chest. "Not like that. I just meant I saw you head out to the dock. Was making sure no one surprised you."

"No one other than yourself, right?" Some of the fight leeched from Logan. He stepped back from the confrontation while keeping Kyana behind him. When he reached his hand out, she grasped his fingers and didn't plan to let go.

"Whatever. I have the internet. I don't need any more porn. Though next time you might want to pay attention, or be a little more discrete. Not that I minded listening." Daryl shrugged. "Going home now. Have a nice night. Tell Ben I said hi."

"You asshole." Logan growled, "Keep the hell away from us. Next time I catch you creeping through the shadows I won't be so friendly, *neighbor*."

Daryl waved without turning. He vanished around a bend in the path. How did he do that?

"Come on." Though the night hadn't cooled off any, Kyana chaffed one of her arms with her free hand. "Let's get inside."

"Good idea." Logan scanned the darkness in every direction as they practically jogged back to the house with their fingers still woven tightly together.

CHAPTER FIVE

"Ben?" Logan joined his great uncle on the porch.

"Yeah, kid." The older man leaned his elbows on the cedar railing while overlooking the expanse of green that united his house with Rose and Kyana's.

"Don't worry, I'll have you home as soon as possible. Everything just as you left it. You'll never know anything happened at all." He slapped Ben on the shoulder.

"Actually, I've been thinking maybe it's time to update a few bits. I saw what you've done so far. You're making great progress on the demolition and it's sort of a blank slate. We should take advantage. Maybe tonight we can sit down and work out a design. Give me your input. Help me invest in some shit that'll up the resale value."

"You're thinking of moving?" Nothing could have shocked Logan more.

"Hell, no. This neighborhood is where I belong. I'm too old for new places at this stage. But you're working on your inheritance kid. Gotta do what's best. Make it your own."

"Jesus. Don't talk like that." Logan scrubbed his face with his knuckles.

"It's just practical." Before they could argue, Ben continued, "So, what'd you come out here for? Need something? Or should I say some*one*?"

Logan cleared his throat. "Sort of. Where's Ky?"

He'd worked like crazy all morning to hit his milestones and free up the afternoon. Being his own boss kind of rocked. He'd planned to use the opportunity so they could hustle somewhere private to put the stash of condoms, which she'd deposited on top of the duffle he'd been living out of since the day after the fire, to good use. Soon he'd have to make a final—more thorough—run to his apartment to salvage what he could before his landlord evicted him. Not much was worth the effort and the gas gauge in his truck had sunk perilously low so he'd put it off. He mentally added a modest hourly pay rate to the list of topics to discuss with Ben later.

After he found Kyana.

Stolen kisses and some ultra-quiet, beneath-the-covers fooling around hadn't come close to satisfying him since she'd blown his mind on the dock two nights ago.

It'd taken him a solid couple hours swinging a sledgehammer after the discovery of the goodies to wrap his mind around the fact that his girlfriend had to buy protection for them because he couldn't afford it. At least she must have realized what the holdup had been without him having to spell out his inadequacy. She'd always been sharp.

Thirty-seven hours had never gone by so slowly.

And now that he'd worked up to approaching her, she was nowhere to be found. Figured.

"Girly headed to Town Hall to search for some records from the holding company Rose and I bought these lots from. I told Ky not to bother. Her friend even said it. Those old papers don't mean jack. Plus that whole office burned down back in the seventies. There's no other information to be uncovered. No funny business with the mortgage. Nothing to do with the Gittlesons and their petition either."

"Rewind a second." Logan tilted his head, thinking of the young couple he'd spotted huddled at the edge of the sidewalk during the fire footage on the news. "I think I missed something. What petition?"

"About a year ago, Laura and Dean made a push to run a ramp to the highway through our backyards. It didn't get very far. All of the other residents voted it down. But there's no bad blood. They followed the process and agreed with the majority. I'm telling you. This whole thing is just bad luck." He sighed. "The world is going crazy. Rose, my house, you kids acting all weird around me. What the hell is going on, Logan?"

"I don't know, but we'll get through it." Uncommon melancholy from his great uncle concerned Logan. He and Kyana had agreed not to pile on another worry by telling Ben they were fooling around with their friendship. After his complicated relationship with Rose, they were afraid he'd be upset. Or object. Neither of them could stand to have their bubble burst when things were bright and new and promising. Although their joint occupancy of her bed had to be raising some questions. The guy was no dummy.

Logan's train of thought reminded him of something Ben had said recently…

"Hey, I've been wondering. What'd you mean the other day when you mentioned sacrificing for your dreams?" He shuffled his boot along a seam in the porch. One board lifted higher than the rest. He'd level it out later.

"It's hard to say anymore what might have been."

"I don't understand." Logan lifted his head, observing Ben's far-away stare.

"I regret a lot of things in my life." He rubbed a gnarled hand over his chest. "Not the least of which is you."

"Shit." Logan reeled at the revelation, something like rejection tearing through his guts. He thought he'd armored himself against disappointment years ago. Apparently not. "I know I was a pain in the ass. I ate a ton and you spent a shitload of money on my clothes and school supplies before you sent me back to my mom each year—"

"If you say one more damn word, I'll show you I'm not too decrepit to put you over my knee or shove my boot up your ass." Ben scowled. "Though you're proving my point nicely. I love my niece, but she didn't do right by you. I could see the damage her selfishness caused and I didn't step up to the plate. Not soon enough. By the time you came to me to stay for that last year, it was too late to fix it all."

"What are you talking about?" Logan scratched his chin.

"You're a damn fine man. The stuff of you has never changed. I could see it in you as a kid. You had a kind heart, you worked hard, and you were loyal to a fault. I should never have let your mom take you away from here at the end of the summers. But I knew I worked too much to be any kind of father figure. Too stubborn. For all of our goods."

"Who do you mean?" Logan squinted, trying to make sense of the rambling self-deprecation oozing from his great uncle.

"Me. You. Rose. Kyana." He sighed. "There could have been something there. All my life, I knew Rose was special. She was the one for me. The only woman I could have loved. I thought she deserved better. I wouldn't accept her help. Some of her enormous inheritance. Hell, I didn't even take her up on the date she asked me on once. I regret every single day that I live on after she's gone, never knowing what *might* have been if only I'd looked past my pride. We could have been a family, Logan. It's my fault you didn't have that. Because of me, you're unsure of the facts I see plain as day. You're a decent person. And you're head over heels for Kyana Brady. Have been since you were old enough to sneak nudie magazines from my shed by the garden."

"Uh... You knew about those?" He scrubbed his face with his hand. "I don't know what to say to that Ben. That's a lot of shit to carry around."

"For us all. I hurt her. Rose. No matter how much I thought I was doing the right thing. I could see it more as the years went on, but I assumed it was too late to change. Too much time had gone by. How stupid. It's never too late to reach for the stars, Logan."

"You sound like a Hallmark card." Logan squeezed Ben's shoulder, hanging on a little longer than man-to-man interaction deemed appropriate. "Don't you fucking worry about me. Not for a second. The time I spent here saved me. You showed me the kind of person I wanted to be. And... Ky and I are sort of working on things. You know, between us."

"You are?" Ben's whole bearing changed. He perked right up and a smile erased his frown.

"Yup. She actually asked me out. I guess she's more like Rose than I realized. We have a date tomorrow night. Reservations at Fleur." He hoped like hell he wasn't blushing.

"Thank god you're smarter than me, kid." Ben grinned. "Want me to stay out late? I think Myrtle is having a bridge game I could join in."

Logan started to deny it, but then thought better of it. "If you don't mind…"

"In fact, I might tie one on and end up staying the night. Yep, that sounds like a damn fine idea. She's offered her couch plenty of times. It looks comfy, too. And I think you might even fit in my suit jacket. It's too big for me anymore. One good thing 'bout not being trendy, you shouldn't be hideously out of fashion."

"Thanks." A million ideas flashed through Logan's mind.

"You got it."

"Hey, Ben. One more thing…" Logan hopped the railing, but paused to look over his shoulder on the way to his truck. "I'm pretty glad right now that I didn't grow up with Kyana as some kind of sister."

Ben doubled over laughing. "That might have been hard to explain to people, huh?"

"Yeah." He cleared his throat. "Still, some bonds are simply understood. You might never have said a thing about it. And maybe you never acted on it. But Rose knew you were connected, every bit as much as you did. There's no way she doubted you loved her. I'd bet our new business on it because I always knew you did. Even before I understood what the words really meant."

"I hope you're right, Logan." Ben sank into the glider on the porch. He seemed smaller than ever, huddled beneath the last golden rays of the afternoon. "But I'll never know for sure. Go to Ky. Make sure she understands."

"I will." He nodded as he climbed into his truck. "I promise."

***

A bell tinkled when Kyana pushed open the heavy door to the brick building that housed their village's records and the lone policeman's office. She stepped into the stuffy building, peeking around the corners. "Hello? Is anyone here?"

"Good afternoon." A woman spoke from behind her.

Kyana slapped her palm to her chest, over her racing heart. She hadn't heard anyone emerge from behind the receptionist's desk. "Oh, Laura. Nice to see you again."

"You too." She smiled sadly. "How's Ben holding up?"

"Eh. He never complains, but I can tell he hates seeing his house in disrepair. I think it helps to be staying in Rose's space though. It's probably comforting, having her things around."

"He's spent enough time there over the years. It's more like an extension of his own place." Laura nodded. "But I'm sure you didn't come in just to chat. Can I help you with something?"

"Would you mind if I asked you some questions?" Kyana took a deep breath. "About the petition you raised."

"Ah, yes. I was surprised you hadn't mentioned it before." Laura wrinkled her nose. "We were new to the neighborhood and didn't really understand what Oak Street was all about. Dean and I are thrilled we lucked into such a tight-knit community. It makes up for the longer commute he has to make, going around town to the other side of the lake."

It was hard to imagine her large, toothy grin as anything other than genuine. "Who else supported the proposal?"

"Why?" Laura hesitated. "Do you think that has anything to do with the fire? The easement right clause expired several months ago. Didn't it?"

"Yes." Kyana nodded. "But I'm wondering if someone didn't realize that. Or maybe they were just bitter?"

"Wow." Laura perched on the edge of her desk then flipped her hair over her shoulder. "I can't imagine anyone going to those lengths. The only other people who signed the petition were new to the neighborhood, I think. I filed a copy in the record storage in the basement. You're welcome to have a look if you want. Fair warning though, it's not very neat down there. Filing isn't my strong suit."

Refusing to ask what other possible job requirements there could be besides answering the phone, Kyana shrugged. "Sure, that sounds good."

"If you don't mind, I actually was planning to leave early today. It's Dean's birthday and I'm making his favorite, duck l'orange, for dinner. Would you lock up behind you when you leave?"

She dug an enormous key ring, complete with at least ten dangly bits, which boasted a variety of cheesy vacation destinations, from her purse and held it out to Kyana.

"Uh, no problem." She jangled the keys. "Don't worry, it's impossible to lose these. I'll swing by and drop them off when I'm finished."

"Maybe just leave them in the mailbox." Laura winked.

Kyana couldn't help herself. She laughed. After charging down here prepared to dislike the Gittlesons, she admitted Ben had been right. They were a little slow to catch on, but nice people. Maybe she'd invite Laura and Dean over to cook out sometime soon. Logan would enjoy having a conversation about something other than bad knees and the best denture cream on the market. Though she had to admit he looked pretty cute hanging out and drinking a beer with all the elderly guys on the block after quitting time.

"You got it. Thanks."

Laura showed her to the basement. The heavy door creaked when she tugged it open. Kyana batted a few cobwebs out of her way then started down the old wooden stairs. "Now you see why I'm not too keen on spending quality time with the records."

"I'm getting a clearer picture by the minute." Kyana flipped on the yellow overhead lights when she reached the cement floor. "I'll make this quick then."

"Okay, I'm out of here. Hope you find something that helps." Laura shut the door with a wave. Her heels clicked on the linoleum above until the front door opened, bell tinkling again, then shut hard enough to dislodge a sprinkle of dust. It rained down on Kyana.

She swiped her hands over her bare arms, imagining the number of spiders per square inch to be similar to the amount of germs in a gas station bathroom. *Blech.*

Either Laura had turned off the air-conditioning or the luxury wasn't a line item in the tiny town's budget. The basement grew stuffier by the minute as she rummaged through stacks of paper, dismissing them out of hand since the top sheets were no more recent than last decade.

Fanning herself, Kyana sidled over to one of the rectangular windows. After standing on a chair and worming her hands around the bars on them, she gave up on cracking the thing open. About nine million coats of paint, probably lead-filled, had sealed it shut.

"Great. Just look faster. Let's move this along." Kyana flew from box to box, trying to gauge which had the thinnest layer of grime on top. One looked a bit newer than the rest. She flipped the top off and grabbed a paper at random. It had a date of last spring.

Bingo.

Leafing through the documents, she came closer and closer to the general time Ben had guesstimated the petition had surfaced. A bead of sweat rolled off her forehead and dripped onto the records, smudging the ink. "Okay, this is nuts," she muttered to herself.

While she was talking, a noise caught her attention. It almost sounded like the bell on the door. Maybe Laura had forgotten something. She decided to haul the likely box upstairs and do more investigating where she could catch her breath, never mind seeing clearly.

The damn thing weighed a ton, but she hoisted it to her hip and began to climb the open-backed staircase. A thump startled her when she was a few treads from the top. "Hello?"

No friendly voice answered this time.

"Who's there?" She continued to ascend, her arms starting to tingle from holding the files. With the box balanced on her thigh, she reached out a hand to turn the knob.

It didn't budge.

"What the hell?" Had the sheriff come in and locked the damn thing as part of his standard end-of-day routine? Had the ancient hardware broken?

Kyana pounded on the paneling, almost losing her balance in the process. "Someone help. I'm stuck in here. Are you there?"

As she strained for any answer at all, she heard it again. The suddenly not-so-sunny ringing of the bell hung on the door. No way could anyone have been upstairs yet not heard the racket she was making. The hair on the nape of her neck stood up straight and her instincts went on red alert.

And that's when she saw it.

A wisp of smoke snaked through the gap beneath the door and rose in beautiful yet deadly formations.

"Oh my god." She almost tumbled backwards. Forcing herself to stay calm, she scurried down the stairs, dropped the box at her feet and hauled her cell from her pocket. Only to see the glaring red X of her no-signal symbol. "Shit. Shit. Shit."

A dull roar above her turned into a pop then a *whoosh*. Dry, old timbers of the floor overhead were clearly visible from her position. They would do a hell of a lot poorer job than the asbestos ceiling tiles Ben's house had contained to prevent the fire from eating through to her hideout.

She raced to the other window, hoping for something different than she'd found earlier. No such luck. Scanning the room, she latched on to the pile of decorations for the front lawn. She dismissed the Christmas tree and the bunny costume but landed on the pitchfork next to the cornucopia and inflatable turkey. That could work.

Kyana grabbed the tool and lunged toward the window. She didn't hesitate to jab the rusted metal at the tiny pane of glass. It surprised her when her first blow glanced off the surface. Exertion combined with thickening smoke to induce a coughing fit. She ignored it.

The next swing cracked the glass and a third busted out several large chunks. A few more had fresh air pouring in. Thank God. Still she couldn't see a way to get past the bars. Who had thought that was a good idea? She supposed city hall had made their own personal fire code. Probably to keep bored kids at bay in their ho-hum town. Petty mischief, like putting the town's Christmas lights up in March, was common when there wasn't much other entertainment to keep teenagers occupied.

Her tank top got yanked upward to cover her mouth. Hell, she was practically an expert at this now. Abandoning her war with the grate, she crossed to the other window and smashed it to smithereens too. Climbing on top of the chair, she stretched her neck, placing her face as close as she could to the outside without risking cutting herself on the wreckage.

"Help!" She screamed as loud as she could manage, over and over, until her throat was raw. The building sat far away from the street and the small shops that lined the block near the town's only stoplight. In the distance, she could see the glowing sign of the pizza parlor and, ironically, the back of the firehouse. No one was around.

The temperature had risen substantially. Sweat began to pour down her back. She glanced over her shoulder just in time to see flames eat a hole in the rafters. Embers plummeted to the floor of the basement and ignited a box of files.

"No!" She dashed toward the blaze, stomping out what she could. For every spark she squashed, another three lit up the dimness with angry red spots.

Fury washed over her. She'd just found Logan again and she hadn't even gotten to fully enjoy the man. She was not about to let some asshole steal the experience of a lifetime from her. No way was she going down without a fight.

Smashing the pitchfork into the grate only cracked the wooden handle, and left her arms vibrating from the impact. She jumped up and grabbed on to the metal, letting her whole body hang from the bars. They creaked. Bouncing up and down, she cheered when one bolt stripped out of the concrete around it.

By placing both her feet on the wall, she gained some leverage. A yank seemed to loosen another corner. Not enough to give her much hope. The fire crept closer, faster than she could ever have imagined, fed by the boxes of old, dried paper.

"Help!" She knew it was pointless, but she screamed again when the heat began to feel intense enough to blister her skin. It wouldn't be long now. Maybe she should breathe in the smoke after all. Passing out would save her from experiencing the horror of burning alive.

A tear rolled down her cheek and she dropped from the bars.

"Kyana?"

It was then she knew she was doomed. She was hallucinating. Dreaming of being rescued by the one man who really mattered. "Logan."

"What the hell is going on? Where are you? In the basement?"

Her eyes snapped wide open. Just in time to see scuffed work boots come to rest outside her prison. "Yes! Yes! Down here. Fire. Stuck. Can't get out. Bars."

"Holy shit." He didn't waste any time. "Step back."

There wasn't much room to move as the flames crept closer, so she ducked. He must have kicked the metal. It rang with the reverberation of his impact. Still, when she peeked up, there were at least three bolts hanging on. Crumbling grey mortar got in her eyes. She blamed that for the moisture dripping from her chin.

The crackle of blossoming flames grew so loud she wasn't sure he could hear her as he hammered the bars again and again with diminishing success.

"Logan. None of this was your fault. You did your best. I'm glad you're here with me now."

"Stop. Talking." A loud bang punctuated each word of his command. "I'm getting you out of here. It's loosening. I can feel it."

"Not enough time." She didn't want him to wonder ever about how she'd felt. "Logan. I love you. I've loved you since we were kids. No one has ever replaced you in my heart. No one has ever lived up to the standard you set. I'm glad we had this time together again at the end."

"No!" His roar would have terrified her if it'd been aimed at her. The next clang seemed ten times as loud. Especially when the bars dislodged and crashed to the floor.

She popped up and stared into his wide-open eyes. Level with her, he'd flattened himself on the lawn.

"I love you too." He swore as he extended his hand and reached toward her.

"Wait. This first." She swung the box of files into his grasp. Before he could argue she shoved. He pulled, tearing some things and spilling others when the box distorted to squeeze through the window. Barely. She figured it served another purpose as shards of glass rained from the opening.

And not at all too soon, Logan's strong hand was back. This time she took it. And held on tight. His other arm reached in and she grasped that one too, locking their fingers around each other's wrists. She didn't have time to warn him about the jagged surface before he hauled her out.

Even if she had, the heat and smoke wouldn't have allowed them to take their time.

A low, keening wail ripped from her throat when a remnant of the window sliced her shoulder on one side. She cringed, but no more pain followed. She writhed, helping Logan thread her through the small egress.

"Almost there, Ky. Hang on. I've got you."

In the distance, men shouted. Several dashed up the hill from the firehouse while others ran back for the truck, equipped with all their gear.

Her feet cleared the window and Logan hauled her the rest of the way up into his arms. She couldn't tell if it was her or him trembling. The world around her jittered as he ran away from the building, onto the lawn. When they'd gone far enough to ensure their safety, he dropped to his knees, cradling her against his chest.

"Are you okay?" He rocked them both, back and forth, until the motion took the edge off her terror. His smell and closeness helped more than she could say.

"I think so." She nuzzled her face into his neck so he wouldn't see the tears she couldn't stop. "Because of you."

"Thank God." His fingers buried in her hair, holding her tight against him. He rained kisses over her head, neck and the side of her face. "What the fuck happened?"

"I don't know." She tried to explain. "Someone locked the door to the basement. Laura Gittleson went home earlier. I was searching for the petition."

"Who the fuck did this to you?" Logan had rarely resorted to anger.

Before she could reassure him, a familiar man approached. The fireman who'd carried her across Ben's yard stood to their sides, arms crossed over his chest. "We have to stop meeting like this. If you want my number, all you have to do is ask. I'd be glad to share."

Logan growled. "I don't think so, buddy. Don't you have a fucking fire to fight?"

"So it's like that is it? I see, I see." The fireman laughed, his palms held outward as he retreated a few steps.

"Could you do me a favor?" she asked.

Logan stiffened until she clarified. "Please grab that box of files by the window before it gets soaked, or catches on fire or everything blows away."

"You got it." He'd jogged over, claimed the records and delivered them to her before she could help Logan come down from his adrenaline high. "Glad to see you're mostly unharmed again. See ya. Duty calls."

Kyana raised a hand when her new friend paired up with another fireman then dashed into the burning building.

"What the hell did he mean by that?" Logan glared at her.

"He was just teasing, Logan. You know, it's not every day I tell a man I love him. *I* wasn't kidding. And it wasn't something I blurted just because I thought I wasn't going to make it."

"Yeah." He swallowed hard. "Same goes. But I was talking about the '*mostly* unharmed' part. Where are you hurt?"

She peered down at herself, taking stock of the various aches and pains the glow in her heart had masked.

At the same time, Logan ran his hands over her. He paused when he touched her shoulder. She squeaked at the stabbing pain that raced down her arm. When he pulled his hand away, it was red. "Shit. You're bleeding. A lot."

He separated their torsos long enough to strip his shirt off. She was glad for the visual anesthetic when he wrapped the cotton around her. Tight. As more and more people joined the crowd, drawn to the black smoke rising—thick and dark—into the evening sky, Logan waved his hand and shouted.

None other than Daryl Thick answered his call.

"You!" Logan glared. "What are you doing here?"

"I passed Myrtle Jansen coming back from the post office. She told me there was a fire. So I came to see if I could help." He lifted a small plastic kit. "I'm trained in first aid from the army, you know?"

"Fine." Logan didn't make her wait for someone else's assistance. "Could you take a look at Ky's arm? She must have sliced it on the window. Sorry baby, I didn't realize when I pulled you out..."

"There wasn't time, Logan." She kissed his frown until it melted away. "You rescued me. If you hadn't shown up—"

They both shuddered.

"I saved myself too," he murmured despite Daryl's presence. "You're everything to me."

They shared another kiss. This one slower and gentler than the last. Kyana nestled deeper into his arms.

"Okay, kids. Enough kanoodling until I get her patched up." Daryl flipped open the lid of his case, snapped on a glove and unwound Logan's ruined shirt. "Damn, you might need a couple stitches. You want to go to the hospital, or should I sew you up here?"

Kyana peered at Logan. "I'd rather stay with you. Do you mind? Will it gross you out?"

"Hardly." He laid his forehead on hers. "I'm not going anywhere, Ky. Not now. Not ever."

"Me either." She beamed up at him.

Daryl's quick administration of local anesthetic and his deft handiwork didn't seem so awful. Especially with Logan to distract her. Before she knew it, the tough stuff was over, reports were logged, and they were heading home.

Together.

CHAPTER SIX

Kyana nibbled the corner of her lip as she stared into her glass. She swirled the remnants of her dessert wine around the bottom of the vessel, entranced by the pattern as she thought back to earlier in the night.

She'd been sitting at Rose's dining room table, the box of files spread out before her, when Ben came into the room. He'd whistled then said, "You look great, girly. Extra girly. You're gonna give my kid a heart attack. Now enough of this nonsense. Go out and have a good time tonight."

He'd waved his hands at the documents she tried to show him, uncaring that she'd finally found the petition. How could he brush off the only clue they might have to the fires?

"I know I'm probably not supposed to talk about the johns at any dinner table, and especially one as fancy as this—" Logan returned from the bathroom, sliding into their corner booth on the same side as her. "But damn. There were a lot of high-quality materials in there. Marble everywhere, a fancy vessel sink and I think the faucet and hardware were even gold-plated. You might want to check it out. Maybe someday I'll get

Nowak Construction to the level where I get jobs like those."

"I know you will." She took his hand and smiled at his enthusiasm, but he was getting to know her pretty damn well. Better than the couple guys she'd dated for close to a year.

"What's wrong, Ky? Am I fucking this up?" His brows drew together. "I'm sure I used the wrong fork, but I didn't think you'd care. That rack of lamb was the best thing I've ever eaten. Well, until dessert anyway. My stomach is full enough to bust. At least it'll go happy."

She couldn't resist leaning over to kiss the last dot of chocolate from the corner of his lips. "Sorry, I didn't mean to spoil your fun. It's nothing you did. I guess I'm just having a hard time pretending like everything is fine when someone tried to kill me. And Ben. I just don't understand what's going on. And..."

"Yeah?" He stroked her hair out of her face and tucked it behind her ear. "Don't stop now. I'm listening."

"I didn't want to ruin our dinner, so I didn't tell you that I found the petition this afternoon."

"You did?" He sat up straighter. "That's great. What'd it tell you? Who was on it?"

"That's the thing." She slumped against his side when he slung his arm around her shoulder. The comfort he infused her with was welcome. "It was pointless. All of that was for nothing. The names were mostly the new people to the neighborhood. You know about the Gittlesons, and a bunch of the other couples that commute to the city. Myrtle Jansen and Daryl Thick and a couple of the crankier residents. Still, nothing that surprised me."

"Were you hoping the bad guy's name would be written in invisible ink on the paper like in a movie?" He knew just what to say to cheer her up.

She laughed, then socked him in the side. "Shut up."

"Ugh. That's not a good idea. I'm already trying to digest faster if I'm going to have my dessert."

"Logun-kun, you already ate yours plus half of mine." She grinned. Watching him scarf the confection had lightened her heart.

"That's not the kind of treat I'm talking about." He leaned in close and nibbled the lobe of her ear before whispering, "We have the house to ourselves tonight. Ben's staying at game night."

"What?" She whipped around to look at him so fast they almost bumped noses. "He is?"

Logan nodded. "Yup. Myrtle said she'd take care of him. Hell, she seemed pretty excited about it. Maybe he'll get lucky too."

Her hand shot up as a waiter neared their table. "Check please."

His laughter, and the squeeze of his fingers on her thigh, had her forgetting all about her worries. With him, she was safe. And she'd let things she couldn't control any more than gravity keep her from enjoying herself for too long.

***

Logan reminded himself for the five thousandth time that he wanted to take things slow. And yet he found himself making out with Ky in his truck in the driveway like they were still adolescents. He'd hauled her across the bench seat and pressed her to his side as they drove. The instant he'd parked, they'd fused together as completely as his fingers had the time he'd gotten epoxy on them as an apprentice. Only this was a hell of a lot more enjoyable.

He searched for any long-lost scrap of propriety he might have in his genetic makeup. Nothing meant more to him than ensuring their first time was special. This was the girl of his dreams. The woman of his future...if his luck held. And he wanted to do this right.

With a groan, he retracted his tongue from her mouth, which tasted pleasantly of the wine they'd shared. She didn't make it any easier on him when she chased him with licks and kisses of her own.

The dazed stare she leveled at him had him sure he was making the right decision. They had to take this party inside before they ended up half-dressed, mashed up against the steering wheel. The last thing they needed was the neighborhood watch bearing down on them when someone's elbow tooted the truck's horn by accident.

"I know where there's a nice comfy bed inside. No rotten old boards or the cab of my truck tonight. Fancy sheets and puffy pillows all the way." He held his hand out to her when he stepped down. She allowed him to lift her and set her beside him. The pleated skirt of her filmy layered dress floated into place around her knees. "Only the best for someone as amazing as you. I wish I could have taken you to a swanky hotel or someplace crazy like Paris."

"Been there, done that. I like where I am right now better. As long as we're together, that's where I want to be." She raised their joined hands to her lips and kissed his knuckles. "Though the thought of getting horizontal somewhere soft and warm sounds pretty fine right about now."

She shrieked when he scooped her into his arms and loped up the hill. He let them in through the back door off the deck then took the stairs two at a time. "That I can do."

They laughed as he spun her around a few times before depositing her on their bed. He couldn't do more than stare when she rose onto her knees. Gazing into his eyes, she hoisted her hem a little bit at a time. Along the way she revealed classic black, lace-top thigh highs held in place by some strappy contraption he couldn't wait to reverse engineer.

An expanse of pale, creamy skin stretched over her belly to the matching bra that cupped her to perfection. And before he could share how absolutely gorgeous he thought she was, she'd abandoned her dress and crawled toward him, her onyx hair cascading off her shoulders onto the bed beside her as she stalked closer.

Powerful, graceful and alluring, she stole his capacity to do anything but react on a basic level.

When she neared, he tipped up her face with two fingers under her chin.

Her smile brightened his world.

"I can't believe that just a few weeks ago, I thought I'd lost everything. And now I have all I've ever dreamed of. Family, home, the start of a business, passion and…you."

"They say things happen for a reason, Logan-kun."

"You're my reason." He didn't need to say more.

She nodded, her eyes shimmering. "Same goes. And you know what else they say?"

"What's that?" Trying to stop her from unbuttoning his slacks or drawing down the zipper would have been ridiculous.

"Where there's smoke…there's fire." She hiked his dress shirt up and nipped the ridge that led from his hip bone, arrowing toward his cock.

The silk of his tie unraveled in a hurry. He couldn't risk her destroying his restraint with the clever fingers that dropped his pants, shoved his briefs to his ankles and cupped his balls in the blink of an eye.

"Damn." He choked when she weighed his sac in her palm.

"That's what I'm saying." She ran the tip of one finger along his entire length. "You seem even bigger tonight, now that I can really see you."

"That fancy petting you're doing certainly isn't making it any smaller." He grunted when she squeezed. "Unless you do it too much. Enough of that."

She gasped when he kicked his feet free of the tangle of fabric pooled around them, then whipped his tie off and twined it around her wrists before she realized what he intended. "Logan?"

The note of uncertainty in her cry had him pausing. "Do you like to be bound, Ky?"

"I don't know. I've never tried it." She flushed, every inch of her turning a pretty salmon color. "I haven't felt comfortable enough to ask guys to experiment."

"That should have been clue number one they were all wrong for you." He nuzzled her jaw, taking the sting out of his rebuke. "But you've thought about it?"

"Yes." She closed her eyes. "A lot. Giving up control isn't easy for me."

"I know." He kissed her eyelids, cheeks and lips gently. "Thank you for trusting me. You're one of the only people who ever believed in me. All the way. I won't let you down."

With no hesitation, she echoed him. "I know."

"Hell, I'll even let you keep your power pumps this time."

"Logan, you like these shoes even more than I do. And that's saying a lot." She smiled before he kissed her.

He stretched her out until she lay completely on her back, restrained hands above her head. The full weight of his body bore down on her.

Kyana didn't squirm. She didn't attempt to escape. Instead she reveled in the heat of their connection, and spread her legs until he sank into the V of her thighs. The moist tip of his cock glided across her thigh, reminding him of practical matters.

One hand shot out to the drawer in the side table and removed a condom from the pile he'd deposited there. After sheathing himself, he went to work on ridding Kyana of the last obstacles to their joining. He'd waited forever for this moment.

If the desperate whimpers emanating from her were any indication, so had she.

It took him a few seconds to figure out how to remove her panties while leaving her garter intact. Though it tempted him, he didn't take the easy way out and rip the packaging off her present. No, he wanted to enjoy the sexy trappings for many sessions to come. Destruction wasn't his thing.

Carefully, he divested her of the scrap of lace, exposing her bare mound to his elevated breathing. She arched upward, presenting him with the perfect opportunity. He couldn't resist tasting her again. The flavor of Kyana had been burning through his palate since their interlude on the dock.

More delicious than their meal earlier, she encouraged him to devour her, preparing to accept him as best she could. While he laved her pussy, his hands snuck upward. They flicked over the front fastener of her bra, making quick work of the clasp. Unwilling to free her from the web they wove together, he yanked the material up, reinforcing the bond made by his tie while leaving her breasts exposed.

No one could fault him for pausing to admire the full yet modest swells and the dark tips that had puckered in the evening air, or for detouring to taste first one then the other. The instant he felt her fingers in his hair, nudging him, he froze.

"Did I tell you to move those hands, Ky?" A love bite on her breast captured her attention.

"N-no." She lifted her arms, placing them near the headboard once more.

"Nice." He kissed her long and sweet.

"What are you doing to me?" She practically panted.

"Loving you." His hips rocked, guiding his full erection along the furrow of her pussy.

"Please. I need you." Kyana tried to align herself to encourage penetration.

He nudged her, but refrained from entering the damp tissue kissing his shaft. Gritting his teeth, he committed himself to enhancing her experience then reached between them. The tip of his cock grazed her saturated pussy.

They both drew a sharp lungful of air.

"Keep breathing." He rubbed his thumb over her lips until she sucked it into her mouth. "Let me inside."

A series of moans and cries encouraged him as he advanced, pressing himself deeper with rocks of his hips until she'd managed to envelop him in her sweetness. Nothing had ever felt so right. He whispered, his face pressed to Ky's neck, "You know, I've never done this before either."

"Hmm?" She sounded as coherent as he felt.

"I've never *made love* to a woman before." He pulled back just enough to stare into her eyes. "Sex never mattered so much."

"Don't worry, I'll be gentle." She craned her neck to kiss the tip of his nose. "At least at first."

Laughter interrupted more kissing as he seated himself to the hilt. When he bottomed out, she rotated her hips, pressing her clit against the plane of muscle at the base of his cock. They locked tight together, perfect counterparts.

At first, he was content to stay there, grinding with her and enjoying the steady pulses that clamped her rings of muscle around him in the most erotic massage of his life. After a while, her kisses grew sloppy and she writhed beneath him with enough vigor he worried she might aggravate her injuries. At least the tie kept her arm out of danger's way as he'd intended.

"Tell me what you need." It wasn't that he didn't know. More that he had to hear it. Had waited a lifetime to live this dream.

"Fuck me, Logan." Decorum fled in the face of their raw, primal lust.

He delivered, fulfilling every dirty encouragement she shouted at him. Thank God they'd waited until they were home alone to unleash their desire.

"I want you to come for me, Ky." He grunted as he picked up the pace, adding a swivel to each thrust, designed to drive her wild.

"No."

Her refusal caused a hitch in his stride. Then a redoubling of his effort. "What did you say?"

"No." She grinned up at him. "Not without you."

"That's not going to be a problem." Electric shocks had been stirring in the base of his cock for a good long while. Hell, she was lucky he hadn't gone off the moment they touched.

He didn't realize it, but he'd modified his strokes. Dots and dashes of an entirely different nature spelled out the way he felt, even if he wasn't quite brave enough to say it and put the best night of his life in jeopardy. Someday soon he'd verbalize the sentiment his cock impressed on her in long and short lunges.

"It's okay to let go, Ky." He stroked a sweaty lock of hair from her brow. "I'm here. I've got you. I won't ever let you down."

"Yes!" She screamed it louder and louder until the clamp of her pussy synched with the cries. The orgasm that washed over her had her milking every last drop of his release from the very tips of his toes. Or at least that how it seemed.

Endless euphoria crashed over them in waves. Each flex of her channel hugged him, eliciting another blast of come. He worried he might overflow the condom for about ten seconds, until he realized he might not care if he did.

And when the violent storming had passed, he collapsed onto the bed beside her, unfettering her hands so they could bask in the afterglow as if it really were a lazy, rainy weekend.

Logan smiled as an aftershock jolted Kyana. He rolled to his back and held her tight, rubbing the tension from her ass, sure that they would have plenty of chances to practice their techniques in slow, gentle sessions. Right after they did this a few dozen more times to take the edge off a decade of yearning.

CHAPTER SEVEN

Logan threw one arm over his head and watched Kyana stretch then push up on her elbows. She swung a leg out of bed. "Where do you think you're going? I kind of liked you where you were."

Understatement of the century.

"I have to pee if you don't mind. I didn't realize this was going to be a sexathon." He hadn't thought it possible, but she was even cuter when she blushed.

Logan rolled over and smacked her on the ass as she sauntered away. "Hurry back."

"I promise." She smiled. "I haven't had my fill of snuggles just yet."

"No problem. I have lots more where those came from." He winked. "And some other tricks up my sleeves too."

"Is that what you'd like me to call it?"

He choked. "Uh, no."

"I like you speechless." She giggled, and he adored the carefree sound on his too-serious lover.

"I have a feeling you'll do that to me plenty. You know, like when I bury myself inside you again..." He pushed out of bed as if to chase her.

"Give me a minute. Then I'm all yours." Her radiant smile brightened his heart an instant before she closed the bathroom door.

Since he was already up, and didn't dare risk falling asleep without her or before round five, he wandered to the window and pushed back the curtains. Not on the side of the room facing Ben's house, but on the opposite wall, near his side of their bed.

Damn, he liked the way that sounded. *Their bed.*

Rubbing the scratches Kyana had left on his chest with those sharp little nails of hers, he peered toward Myrtle Jansen's place, wondering if Ben was really comfortable or if he should go bring his great uncle home. An orange cast to the living room window caught his attention. Was Ben still up at this late hour?

No way had the games gone on this long. Hell, some days the old timers didn't last through the four-thirty episode of Judge Judy, their idol. If someone was still awake, it meant they couldn't sleep. Crap. Kyana would understand if they cut their night short, wouldn't she? There'd be plenty of time later to play. Every night for the rest of their lives, he hoped.

As he debated, he monitored that uneven glow.

And that's when he saw it.

A shadow crossed between Logan's perch and Myrtle's living room.

The bulky silhouette could belong to none other than Daryl Thick based on its size and the fluid way its owner stalked across the lawn.

"Mother fucker." He spun around, nearly plowing over Kyana.

"What's wrong?" The fear that drew lines in her pretty face made him itch to toss some punches. Daryl was older than him by a solid twenty years, but the dude had clearly been trained. This wasn't going to go down easy.

"Nothing. Stay here for a minute. I need to grab something out of my truck." He hated lying to her but wouldn't risk her getting hurt.

"Like what? A tire iron?" She tipped her head. "There's nothing you could have forgotten and your eye ticked. Tell me the truth. If we're going to be partners—"

"Shit. Fine." He couldn't chance stepping wrong now. "It's Daryl slinking around Myrtle's house. It's no coincidence that's where Ben is tonight. I'm putting a stop to this bullshit once and for all."

"Let me call the police." She reached for his hand.

He glanced over his shoulder, monitoring Daryl's progress. The asshole had already crept up to the window and was taking something from a bag Logan hadn't noticed at first. "Go ahead. Notify them, then wait here for me. I think he's up to something and I'm going to stop him before it's too late."

"Be careful, Logan." Somehow she knew better than to tell him not to go.

He dragged on his jeans, shoved his feet in his boots, then kissed her quick and hard. "I'll be right back. Then we'll see about that snuggling, okay?"

"'Kay."

"Love you." The unfamiliar phrase flew off his tongue without hesitation.

"Love you, too." She kissed her fingers then blew the smooch toward him.

Ridiculous or not, he caught it before clomping down the stairs. Doubly pissed off at Daryl, for causing trouble and for interrupting his time with Kyana, Logan channeled all of his anger into sneaking up on the wily bastard. He'd had some experience with this, during those bad judgment years, when his mother had left him to his own devices, sometimes for days or weeks at a time.

When he'd crept as close as he dared in stealth, he launched himself at the dirt bag's legs, tackling him into the juniper bushes.

"*Mufphh.*" Daryl tried to come up with some excuse. It made no sense with branches in his face.

Logan hauled him backward and gave him a nice, solid shake. "What did I tell you about skulking around? Was it you who set those fires? Why? Why are you doing this?"

"Quit your yammering. They'll hear us." Daryl ignored the inquisition.

"Good. Kyana called the cops too. I want everyone to know about all your snooping." Logan curled his fingers in Daryl's black shirt to keep him still.

"I can see she still has her phone to her ear." Daryl might have been lying, but Logan looked anyway. Sure enough, Ky stood not ten feet behind him with her cell and a fireplace poker, watching his back.

"What are you—?"

Daryl seized the opportunity granted by Logan's momentary distraction. The man relied on his skills to evade Logan's hold. The ease with which he broke free made it clear he'd only allowed the illusion of capture to keep from entering a real fight. "Listen to me, lovebirds. I'm not the guy you need to be getting your panties in a bunch over."

"Oh yeah, then who else is out here causing problems?" Logan glared at their nosy neighbor.

"Myrtle." He sighed. "She's batshit crazy. I've known that for years."

"Hell, everyone knows that." Kyana agreed with Daryl, obviously trying to calm him down.

"Yeah, but what I didn't realize was that she's getting more unstable as she gets older. Completely off her rocker and dangerous too. She's the one who's been setting your fires. I've been trying to gather some concrete evidence but she slipped away from me the day of the town hall incident." He shook his head. "I have no idea how. She's wily."

"Are you fucking kidding me?" Logan shook his head. "You expect me to believe we're in danger from an eighty-five-year-old, retired... What the hell did she do anyway?"

Kyana gasped. "She used to work at the Town Hall. Until it burned down the first time. And she won some kind of worker's comp settlement. Rose used to joke that our taxes were hard at work supporting her."

"Seriously?" Logan took his eyes off Daryl for the first time.

"Yeah." The man grunted. "She's always torching shit in that barrel of hers too, no matter how many times Sherriff Collins tells her to knock it off."

"Uh-oh." Kyana added.

"What, uh-oh?" Logan raised his brows.

"One day when I ran out to get Rose's prescriptions filled, Myrtle stopped by. She said she'd watch my aunt while I was gone. When I got back...there was a small fire in the oven." She covered her mouth with one hand. "I didn't think anything of it. Myrtle said she'd tried to heat up something for Rose to eat but there was only a dishtowel in there when I looked. I thought she was getting senile and I didn't want to embarrass her."

Daryl nodded. "It's okay, hon. It took me a long time to figure it out too, and I was looking. I didn't expect the little old lady to be a fucking pyromaniac."

"So what do we do now?" Kyana's eyes glistened in the light of her phone.

"Let's wait for the police and let them handle it." Logan now agreed with her.

"I wish we could." Daryl eased along the edge of the bushes, speaking very softly. "But I'm afraid that glow is getting stronger. And it doesn't look like any kind of lamp to me."

"Son of a bitch!" Logan had assumed his eyes were adjusting to the night. No such luck. Daryl was right. The unsteady flickering was growing by the second.

"Ben," Kyana cried out.

"Shh..." Logan reached for her, hugging her tight to his side. "Let's not give away our advantage. We'll get him out of there, don't worry."

"In all the time I've been watching, I've never seen her with a weapon. Just the silver lighter she carries. I'm willing to risk it." Daryl marched over to the front door, which opened into the living room, where the light seemed strongest.

"No, don't." Logan tried to stop him. With Kyana under one arm, he didn't make it in time.

"Wish me luck." Daryl stepped back and kicked down the door with a smooth move that impressed Logan even as he cringed. "Stop. This is a citizen's arrest."

Logan shoved Kyana behind him, ignoring her protest, and dashed over to assist. When he reached the threshold, his stomach dropped to his feet. Ben stared at him with bugged-out eyes. He thrashed on the couch, trussed up like a calf at a rodeo.

Myrtle hovered above him, humming. She was dressed in a wedding gown that looked almost as old as she was. Had she had it all this time?

A shiver ran down his spine when he realized she was singing the wedding march as she poured gasoline on the floor. Candles of all shapes and sizes ringed the room. It was only a matter of time until the fumes ignited and the whole thing went up in smoke.

Ben grunted and gurgled, no doubt telling them to get the fuck out of there. Pronto.

Unfortunately, he drew Myrtle's attention to them.

"Have you come for the ceremony? I didn't think anyone had gotten the invitations." The toothy grin—complete with several black gaps— she leveled at them froze Logan's heart. "So glad you could join us. Come in, come in."

"Oh, Myrtle." Kyana's sigh was laced with enough pity to tug at Logan's chest.

"You!" Instead of welcoming her, Myrtle became enraged. Logan wouldn't have been surprised if she started foaming at the mouth. "You're not welcome here, Rose. You home wrecker. Trying to steal my man. You've always kept him from me. He's never seen anyone but you. Now that you're gone, he's mine. All mine. Get out! Get *out!*"

As she screamed, she waved her hands, sloshing more gasoline. Logan cringed, hoping the heavy fumes stayed low to the ground long enough for them to escape. Otherwise this place was going to go up like a firework on the fourth of July.

Lacy doilies, curtains, and piles of junk to rival an episode of Hoarders made perfect fuel. They had to get Ben and go. Surely they could fend off one little old lady, even if she was totally loony.

Daryl looked over at him. "You grab Ben, I'll get Myrtle."

Logan nodded. "Three, two, *one.*"

They rushed forward in unison. Daryl leaped the couch in an impressive imitation of an Olympic hurdler. Logan snagged Ben and threw the bound man over his shoulder. When he turned, the horror in Kyana's face caught his attention. Before her scream left her lungs, he felt himself being thrown forward toward the door.

The impact left him shaking his head, trying to put things to right.

Fortunately, it seemed like Kyana and Ben had made it out of the danger zone and onto the soft mulch of the perfectly tended flower beds. They were huddled together as Ky worked the knots free on Ben's ropes then helped him up.

Logan struggled to his feet, spinning to look for Daryl. The man hovered outside a flaming heart, which encapsulated the sofa Ben had been held captive on. Inside the horrifying shape, Myrtle danced. The train of her yellowed dress dragged perilously close to the fire.

Daryl tried to reach her. She spun out of his grasp. A flare up prevented him from jumping across the boundary between them. Instead, he retreated several steps.

"Get out of there!" Logan shouted at their resident hero.

Daryl looked as if he might object until Myrtle lifted the can of gas over her head, drenched herself and gave one final curtsey that turned her into a living fireball. She cackled as she charged Daryl, trying to take him to her own personal hell with her.

"Fuck this." He sprinted for the door, and Logan didn't hesitate to follow.

They left the thick oak standing open.

Myrtle never emerged.

***

Hours later, Ben huddled together with Kyana and Logan around the table in the bright, cheery kitchen of Rose's house. "This is getting to be a habit. Not that I don't love spending time with you kids, but...we've got to quit doing this."

Kyana took his hand in hers and squeezed. Logan did the same for her.

She smiled up at him, hoping they were about to call it a night. Again.

As if he could sense their restlessness, Ben rose. He shuffled toward the stairs and said, "It's a shame about that couch. Myrtle was right. It was pretty comfy."

Kyana just stared at him with her jaw hanging open while Logan cracked up.

"If you don't laugh, you'll cry." Ben shook his finger at her. "And I'm not wasting any tears over that woman. Rose is the only lady who deserved those from us. Have a good night. And for the record, I'm taking my hearing aids out."

Logan looked to Kyana and wiggled his eyebrows.

She climbed into his lap right there at the table and kissed the shit out of him. When they were both breathless, she whispered, "I'd like to cash in my rain check for snuggles now."

"Whatever you like, ma'am." He carried her upstairs to their bed.

EPILOGUE

Six months later

Logan had never been so sure of something, and yet so nervous about it, in his entire life. He paced the sparkling kitchen of Ben's house and snapped the box in his hand open then closed for about the gazillionth time. Inside, a simple antique band nestled inside dark maroon velvet. It hadn't broken the bank—which was shored up by the three jobs Nowak Construction had won after people had gotten sight of his craftsmanship—but something about the delicate scrollwork on the side had reminded him of Kyana.

He stood in the dark for a minute straight, breathing deep and slow. Then he took the flashlight from the countertop in front of him, flipped it on and covered it with his palm.

Dash dot dash.

"K."

He only had to flash the sign three times before the high-powered beam reflecting off her bright-white ceiling roused her. Just like the old days.

Dash dot dash dash. Dot. Dot dot dot.

"Yes?"

A smile crossed his face despite the sweat making his thumb slick on the on/off switch. Now or never.

Dash dash. Dot Dash. Dot dash dot. Dot dash dot. Dash dot dash dash. Pause. Dash Dash. Dot.

"Marry me?"

No light answered his question. His heart tripped in his chest as seconds turned into a minute. He tried again.

Dash dot dash.

"K?"

Still nothing. Had he read her wrong this whole summer? Had he rushed her? It seemed like forever to him but maybe because he'd known what he really wanted from the time he was sixteen. If he screwed it up now, he'd never recover.

He set down the flashlight carefully on the freshly installed granite countertop, switched on the new pendant fixtures over the island, then sighed.

Right before the door burst open and Kyana raced in. She leapt into his arms from several feet away. The force of her advance didn't matter, he caught her easily. Never would he drop her.

"Yes!" She took his face between her palms and kissed him over and over. Between each smack of her lips she said it again. "Yes, yes, yes, yes, yes, yes, yes."

"Mmm." He nipped her lip then set her down. "Let me do this right."

"What?"

"This." He got to one knee on the new hardwood floors and popped open the ring box. "Kyana Brady, you are the only love of my life. Please stay with me. Let's build something special. We've worked on this remodel together, just as we've revamped our relationship into something amazing. I thought it was only right that I ask you to be my wife, here in this house."

"Yes. And yes again." She practically jumped up and down, making him laugh as always.

It made it harder, though not impossible, for him to slide the ring onto her finger.

"It's gorgeous, Logan." She got misty-eyed as she inspected the band.

"I figured you could pick out a diamond. Or maybe something of Rose's to wear with it." It didn't bother him anymore to think of her deep bank accounts. They shared everything. She'd made him see cash was just another one of those. Not the most important one by a stretch.

"I know just the piece." She nodded. "I can't believe this is real. It feels like a dream."

"Stay awake just a little bit longer." He led her toward the counter, where an envelope rested.

"This is for you. Us. From Ben. An early wedding present, he said." Logan waved at the paper, still unable to believe what was inside.

"What?" Kyana peered up at him as she unfolded the deed to Ben's house. "Why?"

"He says we picked everything, it should be ours. And he wondered if you'd let him stay in

Rose's house. Well, he asked to rent it but I already rolled my eyes at him for you."

"It's where he truly belonged, all this time." Kyana sniffled. "Of course, Logan. Rose would love that."

"And so will I." Ben spoke softly from the doorway. "I'm so happy for you both. I feel like this is what I worked all those years for. To have you here. Like this—together. It was worth it. Every minute, every sacrifice."

Logan and Kyana opened their arms and drew him into their circle.

The paperwork shook in Ky's hand. Something fell to the floor.

"What's that?" Ben stooped to claim it. When he saw what it was he froze. "Where did this come from? I put those papers in there myself this morning. The deed was the only thing in there."

Kyana and Logan peered over his shoulder at the bright red rose petal he held clasped in his fingers. They looked to each other and shrugged.

Ben smiled.

IF YOU ENJOYED THIS BOOK BE SURE TO CHECK OUT DIVEMASTERS!

COMPLETE SERIES – 3 BOOKS IN 1

Three SCUBA instructors, who happen to be sexual dominants, are about to take the ultimate plunge. If you're extraordinarily lucky, you'll be invited to join them on The Divemaster, where work and pleasure go hand in hand. Welcome aboard!

GOING DOWN

Archer Banks relishes his carefree lifestyle. Together with friends and fellow divemasters Miguel Torrez and Tosin Ellis, he travels the world, SCUBA diving by day, entertaining lonely female tourists by night. Until his father dies, instantly transforming Archer from a beach bum to a billionaire by shackling him with an enormous, undesired inheritance.

With the help of his family's longtime butler, Archer is determined to turn his new golden handcuffs into a golden opportunity. He prays Miguel and Tosin will come along for the ride when he repurposes his family's mega-yacht into a vessel well-suited for both work and hardcore play.

Never in his worst nightmares does he expect their maiden voyage to be such rough sailing. Not only is Archer's old crush, Waverly Adams, among their passengers, but the men have also stumbled upon a vast sunken treasure—one worth killing for.

Waverly surprises Archer with an alluring naughtiness he never got the chance to experience in their younger days. Busy accepting the challenge she issues his dominant side in The Divemaster's onboard club every night, he might be distracted and short on sleep. But could he also be blind to more dangerous facets of her personality?

When the divemasters can no longer deny there's foul play at hand, will Archer be going down with the ship, cursed by his family's fortune, or will Waverly turn out to be the woman of his most wicked dreams?

GOING DEEP

When her mentor is killed in a lab fire, all his notes destroyed with him, marine biologist Sabine Reynolds is determined to finish his work—a cure for an aggressive form of cancer. She needs a specific coral to continue. To find it, she boards The Divemaster to search the waters around Hawaii.

Crewmember Miguel Torres helps facilitate the collection...and brings out a sensual side of Sabine she hadn't known existed. In the warm tropical waters, she discovers fascinating things about herself and the taboo fantasies she'd never experienced before meeting the sexy guide, who isn't afraid to take charge during their daytime, and nighttime, adventures.

The Divemaster crew come face-to-face with danger in the form of rival researchers, who'll stop at nothing to ensure their success at Sabine's expense. Sabotage, theft, kidnapping, murder, whatever it takes to produce—and profit from—the cure first.

Can Miguel keep Sabine safe and by his side? Or will her enemies put a stop to her research…permanently?

GOING HARD

As the last lone wolf of The Divemaster, Tosin Ellis doesn't plan on partnering up anytime soon. Then his friend Archer commissions an engagement ring for his fiancée…

Jeweler Kahori Akama is sensual, intriguing, and happy to accept Tosin's help sourcing the black pearls she uses in her popular pieces. As their relationship goes from professional to personal, Tosin also learns Kahori's family is being threatened by someone intent on ruining her business to lay claim to its valuable property.

Tosin never expected to find a single woman that could slake his sexual appetites, but Kahori surrenders to her raw and primal urges with the natural power of a typhoon strong enough to blow even a veteran sailor far off course. Once he's experienced loving in the eye of the storm, he can't imagine being satisfied by less.

Once more, the crew of The Divemaster will do what it takes to protect their own. Especially Tosin, who realizes Kahori's heart just may be his home.

EXCERPT FROM GOING DOWN, DIVEMASTERS BOOK 1

Archer Banks's ringing cell trampled the tropical night symphony composed of lulling waves, chirping bugs, and rustling palms. He would have fumbled around on the nightstand to silence the racket if an armful of bronzed, slender woman hadn't stopped him. After rolling the beach bunny off his chest, he settled her gently on the edge of his double bed. Refusing to be distracted by her wild, sun-bleached mane, or the way the moonlight streaming in the window highlighted her damn-near-perfect ass, he forced his dick's attention from the adorable snuffle she surrendered as she burrowed into his lumpy pillow.

Archer turned his back on all that natural beauty. He rebelled against everything in his soul by lunging instead for one of the only remnants of offensive technology he allowed to intrude in his life. He didn't have a choice, really, since the hunk of plastic threatened the integrity of his eardrums by refusing to shut the fuck up.

Only one contact in the entire world had been programmed with the specific God-awful racket that now blared from his phone. The man who was instructed to interrupt Archer's solitude only in a life-or-death emergency.

Fuck. Fuck. Fuck.

Phone in hand, halfway unlocked, he launched himself from the freshly laundered sheets, which smelled of sunshine and ocean spray. He growled to the caller, "Don't expect me to rush to that bastard's side for some kind of deathbed confessional."

Archer figured he maybe should have said hello first. His bitterness had rushed out like pus from a festering wound before he could manage anything else. Odd, since he would have sworn these old injuries were scarred over by now.

"No need. He's gone." The familiar voice on the other end of the line, thousands of miles away, made Archer more homesick than the news of his own loss. "It was fast. Painless. Though probably traumatizing for the young ladies your father was attempting to have sex with when the stroke hit."

"Jesus." Archer stumbled across the room. He slipped out the sliding glass door that led to a half-rotten deck barely big enough for a pair of plastic chairs, then down the three steps to the beach. Naked, he sank onto his knees in the sand. He glanced over his shoulder toward the woman whose name wasn't nearly as memorable as the way she'd sucked him off before getting him hard again, then riding him with thighs powerful enough to cling to a breaching humpback.

Brittany! That was it. He was *almost* sure.

Was he turning into everything he'd spent his entire adult life trying to distance himself from? Had his father remembered the names associated with the assassin pussies that had finally managed to take the bastard out?

Archer's stomach churned at the thought. Acid seared his esophagus. Just like it had before he'd left that world he'd never belonged in. He hadn't looked back since. Not even for a glimpse of the girl he'd abandoned, who wouldn't welcome his attention after what had happened.

This was definitely going to be the second worst night of Archer's life.

"Sir?"

He shook his head when the question came softly—kindly, even—from his family's butler, who'd been more like a true relative than any Archer shared filthy blue blood with. It was the reason he'd borrowed the guy's name when he'd fled and remade himself. "Come on, Banks. You changed my shitty diapers plenty of times. Don't you think formality is uncalled for? I've never been that person. Much to my father's disappointment—"

"Archer." A soft chuckle warmed Banks's tone this time. "That might have been true once. But not always. Over time, I think he might have envied your escape. Admired it, though he was too proud to admit such things. Or maybe he respected you too much to go against your wishes and contact you to let you know."

"I highly doubt that." Archer swallowed hard against the feelings he'd thought he'd buried deeper than a pirate's treasure. He might be a thirty-one-year-old man, but some small part of him would always regret that he hadn't been able to be the son his father wanted.

"Well, this is for certain. He didn't truly disown you. You were never cut out of his will. In fact, despite your wishes, he left you everything."

"Shit! *Everything*?"

"His entire holdings. All of it, down to the last cent." Banks delivered the most devastating news of the night.

Everything Archer had never wanted had finally caught up with him. Golden chains ensnared his wrists and ankles, keeping him from imagining he could ever move freely again. He'd seen firsthand what it took to run an empire.

As quickly as a barracuda snaps up its unsuspecting dinner, Archer had gone from beach bum to billionaire.

Fuck him, life as he knew it—and *loved* it—was over.

He scrubbed his hands through his hair and caught sight of the woman he'd left in his bed dressing hurriedly by the light of the wall-mounted gooseneck lamp before blowing him a kiss and heading for the door.

At least he'd gone out with one hell of a bang.

Literally.

"It's not exactly a death sentence, sir."

"Banks," he growled.

"I mean...*Archie*."

The shock of hearing that long-lost nickname, right now, had Archer blinking fiercely. Somehow he didn't think there was enough salt in the air to blame his reaction on that. "It feels like it. I'm proud of who I am these days. I don't want the money. I don't want to be like him. I can't afford to lose myself."

He scrunched his eyes closed. It was as if he were a recovering alcoholic who'd been offered an entire chain of distilleries. Archer knew unimaginable wealth could corrupt him. It hadn't been easy to sacrifice everything once, but he'd quit superfluous material possessions cold turkey and had never been happier than he was here, with next to nothing.

Good friends, a job he loved, willing women, and time to enjoy life. Those things were priceless.

"So we'll give it away. Form an umbrella foundation that supports any number of charities, funds, and projects for worthwhile causes. A lot of problems can be solved with seven billion dollars, give or take." Banks's solution seemed genius. Simple yet complicated at the same time.

"Perfect. Will you help me? And by help me, I mean run it. Make the day-to-day decisions. I don't need to know the details. Use your judgment."

"Of course. If that's still what you want, after you've really thought about it some," Banks promised. "I am the estate's executor. It will take some time to settle things. Let me see to the legalities, and you start dreaming about who you'd like to help. This fortune could change the world."

"I...uh... Okay, thanks." Archer couldn't believe this was happening. "Name it after yourself. Call it the Banks Foundation."

He had to make sure his father's name wasn't included. No glory for that fucker.

"I suppose that's naming it after *us*, isn't it?" Banks sounded pleased with that. At least he didn't mind that Archer had appropriated his name in his attempt to go incognito.

"Make sure you pay yourself, too. A shit-ton. Ten times whatever you think is an outrageous salary. You deserve a hazard bonus for the decades you've put up with my family's shit. God knows I couldn't do it. As if that wasn't obvious when I bailed."

"I will." Banks laughed, then said warmly, "For the record, I'm proud of you, too. Dream big, Archie."

ABOUT THE AUTHOR

Jayne Rylon is a *New York Times* and *USA Today* bestselling author. She received the 2011 RomanticTimes Reviewers' Choice Award for Best Indie Erotic Romance.

Her stories used to begin as daydreams in seemingly endless business meetings, but now she is a full-time author, who employs the skills she learned from her straight-laced corporate existence in the business of writing. She lives in Ohio with two cats and her husband, the infamous Mr. Rylon.

When she can escape her purple office, Jayne loves to travel the world, SCUBA dive, take pictures, avoid speeding tickets in her beloved Sky and—of course—read.

www.ingramcontent.com/pod-product-compliance
Lightning Source LLC
Chambersburg PA
CBHW071810190726
48292CB00008B/2783